Grïgnyr the Ecordian

A Rewrite of *The Eye of Argon*

By Geoff Bottone

Cover image by Devanath, Pixabay, used under CC0 Creative Commons.

First Printing, 2019

ISBN: 978-1-79-874780-3

Geoffquest

www.geoffquest.com

For Jim,
With Fondness.

-

TABLE OF CONTENTS

FOREWORD

THE BOOK THAT YOU are about to read, while it seems to be a typical and, if I'm being honest about my own writing skills, quite generic example of "swords and sandals" fantasy, has a bit more going on with it than can be assumed at first glance. For you to understand what I'm talking about regarding this story, I'm going to need to tell you another story first.

In 1970, a sixteen-year-old by the name of Jim Theis wrote a novella called *The Eye of Argon*. This work, comprising approximately 11,500 words, was a story told in the vein of Robert E. Howard and his contemporaries. It featured the mighty warrior Grignr, a red-haired, pale-skinned barbarian from the wild lands of Ecordia, who fought and wenched his way across a dusty, inhospitable land to seek a treasure beyond price—the titular Eye of Argon.

Upon completion of his manuscript, Jim put it in an envelope and sent it off to *OSFAN*, a fanzine also known as the journal of the Ozark Science-Fiction society. Grignr's tale of adventure was accepted for publication and printed in the next edition of *OSFAN*. It was accompanied by numerous illustrations made by one Jay T. Rikosh, who also gave Jim's novella *The Jay T. Rikosh Award for Excellence*.

And there it should have ended, except for one very important thing: Jim Theis was, as the story goes, a giftedly bad writer. The story is littered with misspellings, grammatical mistakes, and other errors that should have been—but most assuredly were not—caught and corrected, either during an extensive rewrite or by an attentive editor.

Jim was notable for using words that he only sort of knew the meanings of, leading to unintentionally hilarious malapropisms, or to sentences and scenes that are effectively incomprehensible.

There also isn't much in the way of narrative cohesion or characterization in the story, either. Grignr is a watered-down Conan with the numbers filed off and is, at his core, an unlikeable and uninteresting brute, little better than most of the people he fights. The villains he encounters are usually disgusting, leeringly evil, and, of course, fat. The sole named female character in the piece is nearly naked, annoying when she talks, and serves as little more than a prop and sex object. The other, unnamed, women are either concubines or prostitutes, who are given neither agency nor personality.

Several scenes in the novella have become notorious in certain circles due to their over-the-top ridiculousness. Grignr, for starters, kills the evil vizier *twice*, once at the beginning of the story and once at the end. There is no acknowledgement in the story that there is anything at all weird or plot-relevant about this. Grignr gets most of his blood sucked out by a giant leech, yet he seems to barely notice, and is fine afterward. Most notoriously, after fighting a life-or-death battle with one normal-sized rat (who proves to be the deadliest opponent in the entire story), Grignr pulls out its *pelvis*, sharpens it, and uses it to kill one of his captors.

It is for these reasons that *The Eye of Argon* has become infamous in the fandom community as the "worst fantasy novella ever written." It has been widely distributed and reimagined since its first printing, becoming, among other things:

- the subject of an online *MST3K*-themed roasting.
- a party game in which the participants see how much of the story they can read without falling over laughing.
- charity fundraising events where the audience would bid money to stop passages from being read.
- charity fundraising events where the audience would bid money to force volunteers to read passages for a set number of minutes or paragraphs.

The Eye of Argon came to my attention in either the late 1990s or the early 2000s, recommended to me by people who knew that I was both an aspiring writer and always in the mood for a good chuckle.

The first person who recommended it to me suggested that I check out the *MST3K* version first, since that one broke up the execrable prose with funny jokes and robot shenanigans. I gave that one a go, and I got maybe a third of the way through before getting tired of the *Satellite of Love* sections. I decided to track down an original version of the story and read it straight through.

It was as bad as everyone said it was. I chortled at some of the malapropisms, squinted at some of the misspellings, and tried desperately to make sense of what was going on. I admit to feeling more than a little schadenfreude at Mr. Theis' expense: After all, even if I never amounted to anything as a writer, I could at least take some small solace in the fact that I wasn't this astoundingly bad at it.

And there, my own experience with *The Eye of Argon* should have ended—I had read the terrible story that everyone said was terrible, I agreed that it was terrible, and, now that I was in on the joke, I could occasionally reference rat pelvises, dripping life fluids, and thin, lithe noses to get laughs from fellow nerds.

Except.

I found that, every few years, something drew me back to Google and possessed me to type "Grignr" or "The Eye of Argon" into the search bar. Over the past two decades, I must have read Jim Theis' novella—either in full or in part—about a half-dozen times. Each time I read it, I noticed that my reaction to the work had changed.

I think this was due, in no small part, to my growing maturity as a person, my much more slowly growing skill as a writer, and the fact that I had, in the intervening years, been a participant in more than a few writing groups. What I once saw as simply a thing to be mocked gradually became just another submission by a writer who wanted constructive critique and feedback for his work. During that time, I also learned a bit more about Jim Theis, most notably that the negative reception to *The Eye of Argon* convinced him to never write anything ever again.

When I read the story most recently, in September of 2018, I realized that, far from eliciting derisive laughter and headshaking, the story made me feel extremely sympathetic toward the author and more than a little ashamed. You see, I was once sixteen, and I am sure that my writing attempts at sixteen were just as bad, if not worse, than those of Mr. Theis. Unlike him, I was very fortunate that none of my stories were ever accepted for publication—If I had been, my early work might be as legendarily awful and as thoroughly derided as *The Eye of Argon*. Thankfully, I was spared this, and was permitted to keep on writing, keep my self-esteem mostly intact, and improve my craft. If Jim Theis had had a similar opportunity afforded, he might have had the confidence to keep writing, and might have improved enough to become a competent genre fiction writer. The world will never know.

Also, the idea that *The Eye of Argon* is the "Worst. Writing. Ever," is just a bunch of hyperbolic nonsense. I have read a lot of things since my first exposure to Mr. Theis's novella, and I have to say that it isn't the worst thing I've ever read. It isn't even *close*.

I have read writers who have less of a grasp on narrative structure and pacing. I have read writers who have written far more unpleasant characters and stereotypes. I have read writers who have even less of an idea of what words actually mean or how to use them.

In fact, on my latest re-read, I discovered that Mr. Theis did quite a few things *right* as far as crafting a story was concerned. Don't get me wrong, *The Eye of Argon* isn't well-written, and it isn't terribly original, but, if one can get past the malapropisms, misspellings, rampant sexism, and weird plot elements, there is an actual story in there, as well as some extremely evocative, if lavender-tinted, descriptions.

The basic story is as follows:

- Grignr, a protagonist struck from the Conan mold, defeats some soldiers and arrives in the City of Gorzom.
- While he samples Gorzom's, he is accosted by soldiers, mocked by the city's rulers, and, ultimately, thrown in the palace dungeon.
- After enduring a period of existential despair, Grignr kills a rat, sharpens its pelvis, and uses it to kill the men guarding him.
- He re-arms himself and tries to escape the palace, only to discover a secretive and decadent cult worshipping a blasphemous demon god in the caverns beneath the temple.
- He butchers the cultists, steals the titular Eye from the demon god's statue, and flees to the surface with the cultist's sacrifice.

- On his way to freedom he kills the prince of the city for the first time and the prince's vizier for a second time.
- When he reaches freedom, the Eye transforms into a hideous slug monster. Gringr kills it.
- As the slug dies, it bestows Grignr with an almost Lovecraftian vision of the true horrors of the world. Fortunately, the story ends abruptly after that, so it is doubtful that this vision will haunt Grignr for the rest of his dying days.

That, as swords and sandals stories go, is basic, but not bad. It's a pastiche of the Conan books and movies and, indeed, if one has read or seen the right ones, one can go through *The Eye of Argon* and pick out which ones inspired Jim Theis' work. It isn't original, it doesn't break new ground, but it is perfectly adequate as a story written by a teenager who was inspired by one of the biggest names in the genre.

What the story needed, I felt, was a revision. I had read that Mr. Theis had once considered trying to go back and rewrite his story, using a lifetime's worth of accumulated knowledge to retell the tale of Grignr. Alas, whether because he was dissuaded from picking up the pen again, or whether because he got occupied with other, likely more important, things, he never completed his rewrite. So, I decided—rather pretentiously, I'd imagine—to do what he could not. I decided to rewrite *The Eye of Argon* and to see if I could turn it into a proper story.

I set down a few rules for myself before going into the rewrite. The first and biggest rule was that I would try to keep as many of the characters, settings, and plot elements from the original work as possible. This means is that, yes, Grignr still fights at least one rat and still kills the vizier at least twice in this version. What has changed are the reasons and circumstances around how these elements appear and interact in the story. My hope is that the revision will be similar, if much more coherent and readable, than the original version.

While the plot is, essentially, the same, there have been quite a lot of changes made to the story. Grignr (now known as Grïgnyr) has been made likeable, with more complex and relateable motives. The original's sexism has been dialed way back, most notably the portrayal of Carthena, but also in promoting, "the faithless concubine" that Grignr had angered in the original to the Sultana of Crin. The Prince of Gorzom is now a more complex character, and his double-killed vizier has been made the true villain of the piece. Lastly, the titular Eye has been given a place of greater importance within the story.

I did the best that I could to make the story both presentable and readable by a modern audience, while hewing as closely as I could to the original work. Did I succeed? Did I fail? Was it presumptuous of me to try? That, dear reader, I leave up to you to decide.

GRÏGNYR THE ECORDIAN

By Geoff Bottone

PROLOGUE: THE SULTANA OF CRIN

IN HER BEDROOM, atop the tallest minaret of the grand palace of Crin, the Sultana came all at once to full wakefulness.

Her eyes scanned the room, made ethereal by the drenching moonlight. Her handmaidens reclined upon their divans in fitful slumber, ready to snap awake at a word. Her gelded soldiers, dressed in their woven steel hauberks and iron-ribbed helms, were arrayed in their usual deployment about her bed chamber. The gilded door to the balcony was shut and locked, as was the engraved iron door that opened on the minaret's stairwell. The lattice window shutters were also closed and pinned, admitting the syrupy silver moonlight, the fragrant night air, but nothing else.

And yet…

The Sultana sprang from her bed, her tawny frame as lithe and well-muscled as a tiger's. Her handmaidens, well-trained and desperate to serve, awoke from shallow sleep to assist her with her dressing gown and to kindle the chamber's lights to greater brightness. The soldiers remained unmoving, but their eyes were bright beneath the brims of their helmets, awaiting their Sultana's command.

She allowed her handmaids to drape the silken garment upon her, but waved them away as she fastened its ebon waist cord herself.

"Await my return," she said, though not unkindly, to the handmaidens. To the soldiers, however, her voice was sharp, full of cold command. "You. With me."

The soldiers formed an armored column, with the Sultana at the center, and marched through the door and down the minaret's spiral steps. They processed through long hallways decorated with rich tapestries, across great audience rooms with polished floors, down moonlit colonnades, each step taking them closer to the heart of the palace. As they traveled, they passed other soldiers, both on patrol or stationed at important points. Each one drew themselves erect and saluted as the Sultana passed. She was too engrossed in her own thoughts to return the gesture.

Her soldiers did not question her, for they were mutes and eunuchs both, but the Sultana noted their eyes darting back and forth in their helmets, sending silent, flashing queries to one another as they traveled. Had they tongues, they might have asked, *why is the Sultana awake at this benighted hour?* Or, *where are we going at such speed, when no alarm has sounded?* Or, *what is it that our lady knows that we do not?*

What, indeed.

During their journey, the Sultana had begun to question the niggling fear that had caused her to awaken. Had it just been the after effects of an unpleasant dream? A moment of dyspeptic distress caused by her earlier dinner of sweetmeats? Perhaps an innocuous noise? As they reached the gilded doors of the vault hallway, and the Sultana bid her soldiers to open it to allow her to pass, she wondered if this was a mistake, or merely some wild fancy.

No. It could not be. As she proceeded down the short, carpeted hallway to the inner doors of the vault, their satin finish glowing with a sumptuous luster in the light of the wall-mounted lanterns, she remembered all the intrigues and gossip she had heard in court earlier that day. The rulers of distant lands and city states had learned that she now possessed the Eye of Argol, and so had dispatched treasure-finders, thieves, and sword bravos to win it from her. Her agents had espied an increasing number of foreigners in Crin of late, any one of whom could have been sent to steal the Eye from her.

Not waiting for her honor guard to do it for her, the Sultana seized the handles of the inner doors and threw them open. Within, the vault was as serene and undisturbed as the last time she had left it. The light from the hall glinted off casks and urns of gold, twinkled like starlight on the gems and filigree of a dozen finely made blades, revealed the rich colors in the furs and fabrics piled in sumptuous folds around the room. In the center of this tableau, resting on a plinth that had been made especially for it, stood a polished coffer—the resting place for the Eye.

All seemed well. And yet. And yet.

The Sultana strode across the thick carpet and lifted the coffer's heavy lid. Within lay a small, velvet cushion that bore an indentation about the size of a grown man's fist, but the gemstone that had reposed there did so no longer. The Eye was gone.

Her knuckles whitened against her skin as she gripped the coffer lid. The Eye had been here scant hours ago! The palace, through which she had passed, had been tranquil, its soldiers alert, but impassive! Yet the thief had been here, in the palace's secret heart, and had gone again! How? How?!

She cast her mind back to the soldiers that she had encountered on her journey from the minaret. Might there have been one who seemed a little taller, a little leaner, than the rest? One whose eyes were framed by curious rings of too-light skin? Who bore a straight blade instead of a curved one? Who moved just a bit more swiftly and saluted a bit more hastily than the others that had crossed her path?

The Sultana hurled the coffer's cover into a thick pile of brocaded silk and wheeled around to face her soldiers. They stood in the hallway, awaiting her command.

"There is a thief in the palace!" she cried. "He is dressed as one of you! Find him! Bring him to me!"

I: THE ROAD TO GORZOM

GRÏGNYR STRODE THROUGH THE STREETS of sleeping Crin, scarcely able to contain his dark mirth. He was still arrayed in the accoutrements of one of the palace guards, his red hair twisted into a knot and hidden beneath his iron-banded helmet. Upon his cheeks and forehead, and upon the backs of his hands, was spread a cunning dye of nut oil that made his pale skin as dark as any man of the city-state.

Within a pouch concealed beneath sheathed broadsword and armored skirt, Grïgnyr carried Crin's greatest prize—the Eye of Argol.

There was none to see him in the close and stinking streets of Crin, none to see his hard lips part in a grin as he ducked down a twisting alleyway and made his way to a midden heap. Once there, he stripped off the habiliments of the palace, retaining only the armored skirt, his sandals, and a leather harness, burying the rest beneath the city's waste.

From there, Grïgnyr, his steps buoyant and cat-like, darted along alleys and across shadowed avenues until, at last, the small hostlery at the city's edge city was in sight. He had made arrangements earlier in the day with the elderly purveyor of horseflesh who owned the establishment, traded a pouch weighty with coins for a fresh steed, and left instructions that it be tied up, alone and in the small paddock beside the barn, ready for his nocturnal use.

He saw the horse now, standing close to—and seemingly resting against—the fencing of the paddock. Its head was down, nose close to the ground, and its back was swayed in the middle, as if it was not strong enough to bear up even its own weight. As Grïgnyr had carefully chosen the horse earlier that day, seeing its strange posture now gave him pause. He drew his heavy blade from its scabbard and approached the paddock, and it was not long before the unmistakable stink of blood reached his nose.

The horse was dead, slain but a short time ago by a knacker's club and trussed up against the paddock in a crude parody of a living horse. Grïgnyr's heart went out to the beast, for it had once been as wild and spirited as he, and one of his reasons for purchasing it was to give it free rein to once again gallop across the high desert outside of Crin's stifling walls.

He reached out with a gentle hand and patted the creature between its shoulder blades, sending a quiet prayer to Myrk that the horse be received eternally into that grim deity's keeping.

It was a trap, of course. Only Grïgnyr's keen senses and his panther-like stealth had, so far, prevented him from springing it. He glanced around at the ramshackle tenements, the reeking tannery, and the house of ill repute that hemmed the paddock in on all sides. They should have been teeming with life, even at this late hour, but all were equally dark, silent as tombs. He peered into black windows and shadowed alley mouths, straining to see the foes he knew must be lurking there.

Grïgnyr knew that Crin's eastern gate was but a few streets away, and he knew that whoever waited in the shadows had neither seen nor heard him, else they would have sprung. He knew that he could withdraw, travel east, and escape the terrible city and its defenders. In but a few moments, he would be free and away across the great desert.

And he would have done so, had it not been for the horse.

Shouting a mighty oath to Myrk, Grïgnyr swung his blade. The keen edge struck the bands of rope that held the horse imprisoned against the paddock, parting them all with a single blow. The horse, released from its bonds, slumped and toppled onto the paddock's hard-packed earth, its final breath fleeing its lungs in a long, loud sigh.

At once, the mounted eunuchs waiting in the dark recesses about the hostlery set spurs to their horses' flanks, surging forward to encircle Grïgnyr in a tightening noose. Swift though they were, the barbarian was swifter still, already halfway through a narrowing gap between the commander's horse and the horse of one of his subordinates. Both swept their curved blades down, crossing them before Grïgnyr to bar his way.

Grïgnyr's broadsword flashed once more, hewing the subordinate's arm off just above the elbow. The eunuch let out a ragged, tongueless cry and toppled backward off his mount, gore spraying from the awful wound.

Seeing that the soldiers had almost trapped him, Grïgnyr seized the reins of the now unmanned horse and, with one smooth motion, stepped into the stirrup and vaulted into the saddle. As he brought the horse around in a tight circle, the commander rained desperate blows down on him, hoping to kill him or prevent his escape. He parried these frantic attacks with easy grace and, when his foe drew back his sword to launch another assault, Grïgnyr smote a mighty blow against his helm. The commander slumped forward against the strong neck of his mount, and Grïgnyr, choosing not to waste another look or strike at the man, dug his heels into his horse's sides, riding with Hell's fury toward the city gates.

*

In the last hour before dawn, a simpering courtier, his robes drenched with sweat, entered the Sultana's throne room and prostrated himself on the floor before her. He did not have to look upon her countenance to know that she was angry, and he knew that the news he brought would do little but enrage her further.

"Well?" said the Sultana at last.

Keeping his head down, he forced the words from his dry throat. "He has escaped, Sublime One. Out the eastern gate. A short time ago."

The courtier heard the sharp sound of the Sultana drawing breath, as keen as the edge of the executioner's sword. He clenched his hands and chewed on his lip, waiting for the Sultana's divine wrath to fall.

"Awaken the scribes. Tell them to send word of this grievous insult to my honor on ravens' wing. Though I am loath to have the Eye fall into the hands of my neighbors, this upstart must be punished."

The courtier swallowed as a cold sweat beaded on his brow. He knocked his head on the floor three times and withdrew from the Sultana's august presence, glad to be carrying her message to her scribes, gladder still to have survived her anger.

*

Grïgnyr had dismounted some time ago, and led his exhausted mount along a winding, weather-beaten trail that cut a dry, shallow groove across the high desert. This was a barren place, a wasteland bordering the great Norgolian Empire. The Norgolians respected the nameless desert, but had no need of it, and no other prince or nation was desperate or fool enough to lay claim to it. And so, it remained empty and unsettled, except for well-armed merchant caravans, bands of sun and wind-hardened bandits, the occasional mad or divinely-touched prophet, and now, Grïgnyr.

His first hope had been to travel by night, but word of his daring raid on Crin's palace had preceded him, and he had been set upon by all manner of avaricious mercenaries and cutthroats. Knowing that they would not cease their pursuit, Grïgnyr kept on traveling day and night, putting his stock in a second hope—that they would not be so overcome with greed that they would waste themselves or their steeds following him.

And now, with the noonday sun beating down upon his head with all its infernal wrath, Grïgnyr realized that he had another hope, for the water skin strapped to the saddle of his new horse had been exhausted half a day before, and though the rippling air around him suggested numerous low-lying places filled with life-giving drink, Grïgnyr knew that they were but mirages. His third hope, then, was to find one of the true oases of the unforgiving desert or, failing that, to reach Gorzom before his thirst or his pursuers overtook him.

His horse, plodding next to him, wheezed and panted in the blistering sun. Grïgnyr stroked the lagging beast's neck and gave it a look of sympathy. He knew that he could do no more for the horse, having stripped it of its heavy saddle and other trappings several hours ago. He had also left much of his own equipment half-buried in the desert sands, both to make his burden lighter and as a relief from the desert heat. He now wore only his sandals, the leather harness, his loincloth, and his sword. The Eye was still safe, hidden from the baking sun in a pouch dangling from his sword belt.

Grïgnyr was heartily glad for one possession of which he had not, initially, taken stock. This was the nut dye that had, temporarily, given him skin the color more like that of the peoples of Crin. It remained on his skin, despite the abrasive winds and the constant soaking of his sweat, providing his normally pale flesh some protection from the sun's merciless rays. He would have been well-roasted and in agony long since, had he not anointed himself with it.

And so, thus arrayed, man and horse plodded across the desert, their feet heavy, their heads downcast. Both the horse's mane and the long, fiery red hair of the man hung limp about their faces, slick with sweat and caked with dust. But, although their hair was still damp, their skin beneath was dry, and no beads of moisture issued up from their pores. What the horse thought of this cannot be known, but Grïgnyr knew enough of the world and its mysteries to know that it was a harbinger of impending death. He had his third hope now, and nothing else. If they could not find water soon, both he and the horse would die.

How long they progressed in this fashion, Grïgnyr did not know, but after a time, he became aware of familiar sounds being carried to him by the desert wind. He gently halted his former mount and fellow traveler and, when the horse at last stood still, cocked an ear and listened intently.

Yes, there was no mistaking it. Another horse, perhaps more than one, galloped down the twisting path toward him. He could pray that the rider was friendly, a fellow traveler, or an advance scout for a caravan, but the horse moved with such reckless speed that Grïgnyr knew such prayers were in vain.

Grïgnyr turned, squinting behind him, watching as a growing cloud of dust announced the nearing presence of his pursuer. With a sigh and a silent oath to Myrk, Grïgnyr gave the horse another friendly pat and a scratch between the ears.

"My friend," he said. "I hate to do this, for I know you are as taxed as I, but I must ask that you bear my weight one last time."

The horse snorted by way of response, and Grïgnyr gave a grim laugh.

"I do not gainsay your disgust!" he said, eying the growing dust cloud, "but know that, no matter how we fair in this encounter, you will only carry me briefly. Now, are you ready, my friend?"

The horse tossed his head and Grïgnyr, believing that the beast had given its assent, took a firm grip on the reins and swung himself up onto its back. The horse's hide radiated such intense heat that it all but scalded Grïgnyr's thighs.

Before long, the shapes of two riders and their horses began to resolve out of the cloud of dust. They were men of Simar, and mercenaries besides, judging by their flowing silks and the gold-chased edges of their armor and shields. The thick brims of their heavy helmets cast deep shadows over their eyes, and their mouths were set in cruel, hard lines. Both men were streaked with dust and sweat, and their overtaxed horses had worked up a rich lather struggling against the desert dryness.

The mercenaries reined in their mounts, halting a short distance away from Grïgnyr. One of them managed a smile and a dry chuckle. The other said nothing.

"You have led us on a merry chase, barbarian," said the first, "but we have caught you at last."

"Not yet," said Grïgnyr, baring his teeth in a fearsome grin. "So far, you have only found me."

"Brave words," laughed the first mercenary. "Brave, but empty. Look at yourself, barbarian! You are half-dead already. We do not even need to lay a hand upon you. In a few hours, the desert will have done all the work for us."

"Then why risk your steeds?" asked Grïgnyr. "Why risk yourselves? Why not cower behind the horizon and wait for me to fall?"

"Because we have no particular enmity with you," said the first. "You are a man much like us—a sellsword, a vagabond, who was brave enough to enter the palace of Crin and make off with its greatest treasure. We wished to pay you our respects, and to save your life—for it does very much look like it needs saving. Will you allow us to help you?"

"For what price?"

The first mercenary laughed again and plucked a fat skin of water from off his horse's saddle horn. "For the Eye, of course!"

"Never."

The second mercenary laid hand on his sword, but the first only tutted, as if in disappointment at an unruly urchin.

"My friend. Please. See reason. The Eye of Argol is a great treasure, certainly, but it is valueless compared to your own life. Give it to us and we will give you anything you need—water, food, silks to ward off the sun. We will leave you here, alive, and return to Crin with tales of our titanic battle. Once there, we shall collect our reward from the Sultana, go forth in wealth and splendor, and never lay eyes upon you again.

"I know it is hard to bear," the Simarian continued. "You possessed the desert's greatest treasure, only to lose it. Think on it this way: you will still be alive, and free, with all the treasure vaults of the world still to plunder."

"You soft, civilized folk may be able to live with such deceit," said Grïgnyr, shaking his head, "but I cannot. I would sooner die here than live on as a liar and a coward."

The first mercenary shrugged. "Very well, barbarian. You leave us no other choice."

"I know it," said Grïgnyr, readying his blade.

The second Simarian drew out his curved sword, and it flashed in the noonday sun as if it were aflame. He spat upon the ground and, for the first time, spoke.

"Prepare to embrace your gods in the afterlife, Ecordian!"

"Die well, and may Death herself kiss you," replied Grïgnyr.

The three horsemen spurred their mounts forward, meeting in a roaring clash of metal, sand, and dust. The Simarians were well-trained in the art of the sword, better by far than the eunuchs that served as the elite guardians of Crin, and it was all Grïgnyr could do to keep them from beating past his guard. He gritted his teeth and grasped his sword in two hands, absorbing blow after blow. Beneath him, his exhausted horse staggered under his weight and the ferocity of the assault, and Grïgnyr feared that it would collapse beneath him.

Round and round they went, men and horses, their blades flickering like lightning in the sunlight. And though it seemed, by all accounts, that Grïgnyr would go down beneath the curved swords of the Simarians, he found the will to endure their unrelenting assault. Grïgnyr drew upon reserves of strength he did not know existed—perhaps sent to him in his final hour by hoary-bearded Myrk himself, or perhaps it originated from his anger at the thought of dying such a lowly death in such a terrible place.

Whatever the case, Grïgnyr's rage was such that it soon allowed him to overmatch the mercenaries in both speed and ferocity. Rather than simply weathering their attacks, he now began to fight back with ringing blows of his own. The Simarians swiftly gave ground, and Grïgnyr, seeing his opening, let out a bloodcurdling howl and swung his broadsword with all his terrible might.

The first Simarian let out a tortured death cry, clutched at the gaping wound in his stomach with bloodied hands, and toppled from his saddle to writhe in agony upon the desert hardpan.

"Damn you, barbarian!" roared the second mercenary.

For response, Grïgnyr leaped from the back of his horse, seized the second Simarian by the neck of his hauberk, and dragged the man bodily from his mount. The two struck the ground hard enough to knock the breath from Grïgnyr's lungs. As he struggled to regain his breath, the mercenary pinned him to the sand and raised his curved blade for the final blow.

"To the black pit with you!" the Simarian screamed.

Grïgnyr, fast as lightning, snatched a leaf-bladed dagger from the mercenary's belt and thrust it upward into his unprotected throat. The man gurgled as he died, disgorging a bubbling shower of blood upon Grïgnyr's face and torso.

Grïgnyr rolled the dying mercenary to one side, arose, and fetched up his sword. Then, with two precise thrusts, he brought swift and honorable deaths to those that had pursued him.

"May Myrk look fondly upon you as you reach the gates," he said, before spitting a gobbet of the mercenary's blood upon the sand.

As silence once again descended upon the desert, Grïgnyr padded off after the dead Simarians' horses, seeking only the fat water skins tied to their saddles.

II: ILL-MET IN GORZOM

THE WATCHER HAD WAITED at Gorzom's western gate of for three days. On the evening of the third day, as the sun set, red and bloated, along the western edge of the desert, she was rewarded for her vigilance. As the shadows lengthened, merging with the growing darkness, a strange procession came into the watcher's view. She spied three horses—tired, but well cared-for—with only one rider between them.

That rider was a curious sight in his own right, piebald in both equipage and physique. Even in the dying rays of the sun, his skin was a curious mottled pattern of dusty brown, sunburned red, and the pale shade that denoted someone from wetter, northern climes. He was garbed in mismatched clothing and armor, seemingly picked at random from Crinish and Simarian lands, though he was armed with a long, straight sword of a design foreign to either city-state. He sat tall in the saddle, taller than most men, and was ornamented with a fine, long plume of crimson hair that smoldered at the same intensity as the sun.

It was common in Gorzom for the gates to be shut the moment the sun vanished from the horizon, and so it appeared that the rider had reached the city at a most opportune time—any later and he would have been forced to encamp outside the walls of Gorzom until the morrow. The watcher, however, cursed her luck. Had the rider been delayed, it might have forestalled the machinations of those in the city for a few, precious hours, and given her time to enact her own plans.

But she could not think on that now. She had much to do.

*

The rays of the setting sun stretched before Grïgnyr, illuminating his approach to the city with a carpet of smoldering red and gold.

He found, to his surprise, his spirits lifting at the sight of Gorzom's ancient walls. As a free-born man of Ecordia, he normally had little use for cities, with their filth and their contemptuous stewards and their corruption, but he found this opinion somewhat changed by his long excursion across the desert that protected Norgolia's southern border. Though Gorzom would possess such features that were distasteful to him, it also promised respite from his journey, offering food, baths, wine, and wenches to satiate and sustain him as he traveled onward to more hospitable climes.

He arrived at the western gate just before the guardians of the city heaved it closed, and they begrudgingly halted in their duties so that Grïgnyr could enter ancient Gorzom. Once within the city, he found a stablemaster whose stock suggested him to be a man skilled at maintaining horseflesh. Grïgnyr parted with some coins taken as plunder from the Simarians and informed the man, in no uncertain terms, that all three of his horses must be well-cared for until his eventual return. The stablemaster blanched at the sight of Grïgnyr's mighty thews and stammered an assurance that all would be well with his mounts.

From there, Grïgnyr proceeded to sell off such accoutrements taken from the Simarians that he did not need, thereby adding to his store of coin. He then procured for himself such garments that would keep off the desert rays and allow him to better blend in with the Gorzomi, inquired until he located an inn with a reputation for wildness that matched his own, and then traveled there to refresh himself from his long journey.

It was nigh on midnight before Grïgnyr had been bathed, fed, and watered. In his new garments, with his broadsword on his hip, and with the Eye of Argol stashed away beneath his raiment, he ventured into the common room of the inn. It was not long before he had found a table and a steady supply of wine, thereby allowing himself to fall into a haze of drunkenness and merriment.

In one corner of the large room, enshrouded by lantern smoke and thick with the smell of fragrant drink, a band of Gorzomi in outlandish costuming played music on giant hide drums and on great fifes of bone and horn. Though the music was foreign to him, there was something in it that was primal, recognizable, that stirred the bloodlust in Grïgnyr's warrior heart. The music, thrumming and loud, all but drowned out the raucous laughter and shouted conversation at the nearby tables.

If Grïgnyr had dared to close his eyes in such a place and focus solely upon the music, he could almost imagine that he stood alone in the vast and cavernous hall of Myrk, listening to the eternal song that announced the newly-arrived dead.

Indeed, it seemed that Grïgnyr was not the only one moved by the music, for more than a few of the revelers, tipsy from drink and impelled by the beat, leapt to their feet and danced themselves into a frenzy. Amidst this chaos, the serving girls threaded their careful ways, bringing small amphorae and cups to any table that called for them. As he observed them, Grïgnyr noted a peculiar custom. If the patrons at a table favored a serving girl, they would clear a space amidst their cushioned seats and bid the lady sit, paying her for the privilege of drinking—and sharing her amphora—with them.

One such serving girl now approached Grïgnyr's table, delicately shouldering her way past a rowdy band of sword bravos. She was slim and dark-skinned, clad in the diaphanous and spangled silks that were the common uniform of the wenches of the inn. Her hair had been dyed the bright color of orchids; it drifted, smoke-like, behind her, floating effortlessly in the room's torpid air. As she drew closer, Grïgnyr noted the strong, smooth musculature of her legs and arms, the old, pale scars that crisscrossed her skin, and the alert and chilly hardness of her piercing blue eyes. The sight of all these together made him sit up upon his pile of silken cushions as the wench bent down and offered him a pour from her amphora.

"You seem different from the usual fare," said Grïgnyr, stretching out his cup to her. "These other girls have been made soft and indolent by civilization, but not you. You…"

"Be silent, Ecordian," she hissed, even as the wine sloshed into his cup. "I have come to bring you warning!"

The strangeness and suddenness of her reply silenced Grïgnyr. He waited until she had finished her pour and then set his full cup on the table before him. Looking around to see if anyone had taken undue notice of either himself or the woman, Grïgnyr flashed a vast and toothy grin and bid her take a seat. She did so, quickly and a touch too furtively, setting down the amphora in such a way that it served as a small, clay shield between herself and the rest of the room.

"Who are you?" asked Grïgnyr, maintaining his smile. "And why have you come to warn me?"

"I am Carthena," she replied, "and I know what you brought with you out of the palace of Crin."

Grïgnyr reached for the hilt of his sword. "If you seek to take my prize from me, woman, it will not go well for you."

"No!" Carthena shook her head angrily. "Listen to me, fool! I have no desire to possess that which you carry, unless it were to bear it as far away from here as possible."

"Then why seek me out?"

"To give you warning, as I have said." She leaned forward, transfixing him with her icy eyes. "Listen well, Ecordian—I know about your prize, but I am not the only one who knows. There are many here in Gorzom who have received word of your coming, and who know what you have brought with you across the desert. Some covet it for its value, but others desire it for more sinister…"

A shadow loomed over the table, blotting out the lantern lights. Grïgnyr leaned back as an iron-shod boot lashed out from the sudden darkness, striking his wine cup and sending it flying against the wall. The wine within it sprayed outward in a crescent, anointing the numerous pillows with dark stains.

"What is the meaning of this?" shouted Grïgnyr, his mighty muscles coiled to spring.

The owner of the boot, a Gorzomi dressed in the uniform of the palace guard, leaned forward and smiled an ingratiating smile at Grïgnyr. The light of the tavern lanterns played across his teeth, sending up a twinkle from the bits of gold scattered amongst the ivory. The man then placed a booted foot upon the damp table and leaned toward Grïgnyr in a gesture of seeming camaraderie and good cheer.

The music stopped, and Grïgnyr saw several of the folk of Gorzom—patrons and musicians alike—fleeing out into the chill desert night. Perhaps a dozen others, and these were identically attired to the guardsman, arose from their tables around the inn and moved toward the sudden commotion.

Carthena adopted the mien of a humble serving girl and sought to leave the table. The man's voice stopped her.

"You will remain where you are, girl, or you will die."

He then spoke to Grïgnyr, his voice taking on a softer tone. "A thousand apologies for the intrusion my friend. We have been tracking this sneak thief for many weeks and now, at last, we have caught her."

"She is no thief," said Grïgnyr.

The guardsman's laughter was cold and flat. "My friend, you only say that because, most fortuitously for you, we have caught her in the act. This comely wench earns her mark's trust with her charm and intrigues, before drugging him with soporific-laced wine and looting him of everything of value. Indeed, had we not sprung our trap, you would soon have been picked as clean as a desert corpse."

"She is no thief. Leave her be."

The guardsman clucked his tongue and shook his head. He spoke again, and this time, it sounded as if he addressed an idiot child. "Such rudeness! And from a man newly rescued from this wench's intrigues!"

He smiled, and now it was as if Grïgnyr beheld a viper's fanged grin. "An outlander...newly arrived and with no ties to mighty Gorzom. Hmm! Perhaps I have misjudged you, sirrah! Perhaps you are not the innocent that I took you for, but a lowly villain in league with this woman here, who, between you, seek to rob the innocent and prosperous of this fair city."

"Liar!" shouted Grïgnyr.

"We shall leave that to the prince to decide," said the man. "You are both under arrest. You will come with me."

"He is innocent," shouted Carthena all at once, "and a well-meaning fool. I am guilty of the charges. I will go with you, but please allow him to go free."

"I do not think so," said the guardsman.

"You will leave us *both* be, city dog!" said Grïgnyr. "Or, by Myrk's hoary beard, I shall refill my wine cup with your blood."

The guardsman, his smile vanishing, removed his foot from the table and stepped away. At the same moment, the cohort of palace guards moved to surround the table, weapons naked and glinting in their hands. The guardsman glanced around and, seeing that he had the support of his companions, plucked his own blade from his wide, purple waist sash. As the bronze blade cleared the sheathe, Grïgnyr noted a symbol like a lidded eye carved upon the tang.

"You are welcome to try, Ecordian," said the guardsman, laughing.

"No, Grïgnyr!" shouted Carthena. "There are too many!"

But Grïgnyr was already rising, his warrior's blood running hot in his veins. No one who besmirched the honor of his companions, or spoke falsehoods about him, or questioned his skill with axe or blade or bow could be allowed to go away unanswered. With a mighty heave, Grïgnyr drew his broadsword. He faced down that contingent of the guardians of the palace, confident in their numerical strength, protected by hauberks of riveted mail, and roared a battle cry that shook the inn to its rafters.

He rushed the garrulous guardsman and smote him with a blow that would have crushed his skull had not the other blocked with his slender blade. Even still, the man's crescent of bronze could not turn aside the full force of Grïgnyr's attack, and he collapsed, an ugly, bloody gash marring his scalp.

The others rushed in to avenge their leader, hemming Grïgnyr in on all sides and harrying him with bronze blades, axes, and short-handled spears. Grïgnyr drove them back as best as he could, but he was as a bear overpowered by a pack of alpine wolves. They pricked him in a dozen places and, at last, pushed him over the table. He fell, and though the many cushions scattered around the table caught him as he collapsed, Grïgnyr dealt himself such a blow to the head upon the inn's tiled floor that his consciousness was rattled from his grasp.

As the darkness descended, he thought he saw Carthena, her wrists being bound by the guardsmen, frowning and shaking her head.

"Fool," he thought she said, her voice laden with sorrow. "Brave, barbaric fool."

III: THE PRINCE OF PLEASURE

GRÏGNYR STRUGGLED TO CLEAR his addled brain as he drifted between oblivion and wakefulness. As time passed, his periods of awareness grew steadily longer, until he was, at last, aware of his surroundings.

He found himself flanked by two of the palace guard, each of whom had thrown one of Grïgnyr's well-muscled arms across their shoulders. The duo struggled beneath his prodigious weight, but aside from the occasional grunt, did not complain at their labors. At Grïgnyr's front and rear marched some of the palace guard that had accosted him at the inn. Their leader occupied the place of honor in the vanguard, hastily-bandaged head held high.

As he was dragged along streets and up steps, Grïgnyr blinked his eyes, shook his heavy, battered head, and tried to take stock of his surroundings. He realized, after a moment, that Carthena was not with them.

Grïgnyr thought that he remembered a tableau, in which scratched, bleeding guardsmen held a snarling, gnashing Carthena as they might have held a wild cat. Through the haze, he recalled a single barking order by one attempting to staunch his forehead wound with a ragged bit of cloth.

Grïgnyr hoped that her fate was better than his own. Looking down at himself caused a wave of pain and nausea to wash over him, but also confirmed what he had feared—the guards had stripped him of his new clothes, leaving him naked apart from his loincloth and sandals. His sword was also gone, though not far, for it hung on the leader's hip beside his own blade.

Worst of all, they had found and taken the pouch he had hidden beneath his clothing, and with it, the priceless jewel—the Eye of Argol!

"Heathen dogs," he shouted, struggling against the strength of his handlers. "Give me back what is mine and turn me loose, or it will go hard with you."

The guard captain raised his fist, bringing the procession to a halt. He turned, glaring at Grïgnyr with a baleful eye, and Grïgnyr realized that the cloth that bound the man's bloody head had been torn from his stolen clothing, bought just a few scant hours before.

"It would be wise of you to hold your tongue, outlander," said the captain. "You go now to meet Agaphim, the prince of the city, who will decide your fate. If you show him proper deference, he might be lenient with you."

"I kneel to no man!" roared Grïgnyr. "Especially not the pampered and preening princes of civilization. Release me at once, or I shall…"

"You will be silent!" shouted the guard captain. "Do not force my hand, outlander, and make me order my men to clout you into submission. You have suffered a grievous blow this evening, and you are lucky to have recovered. Another might kill you."

"The same," said Grïgnyr, "could be said for you."

Now the captain smiled, but there was no mirth in it. "Indeed. Your blow was well struck, outlander, I will grant you that, but I assure you that you will not be given the opportunity to strike again.

"Out of respect for your great prowess, I will tell you this, hold your tongue as you approach the palace and, if Sargoth is kind, the prince might spare your life."

At the mention of Sargoth—presumably the city-dwellers' soft perversion of a deity—the guardsmen around him snickered and exchanged glances, as if sharing in on a clever jape.

Grïgnyr, still trussed between two of the guards, regarded his captors with an angry glower, but spoke no further words. Though he hated the men that held him, he knew that escape was, for the moment, impossible, even had he had his blade and all his wits about him.

As he prayed to Myrk to deliver him from his shameful fate, Grïgnyr was dragged up the hill that overlooked the city, and to the gates of the palace that sprawled across it. The soldiers brought him through gilded entry portals, both ajar and unguarded, and into an overgrown garden whose appearance was made even more wild and primeval beneath the moon's radiance.

His captors carried Grïgnyr along passageways and through galleries reeking with the acrid stench of sweat and debauchery, and which, though richly-appointed, seemed to have fallen into disrepair. Here and there, he saw that the once fine furnishings were laden with detritus and the somnolent, half-naked forms of numberless palace-dwellers.

Grïgnyr was dragged past the entrance of the palace's chapel, and through it he beheld the dust that had settled on the altar goods and worn, wooden kneelers. He also saw the bas relief of an open-palmed hand—presumably the sigil of the god Sargoth—had been crudely defaced with chisels.

At last, they brought him into a large, round room, lit by smoldering braziers and clouded with a miasma of perfume and lotus blossoms. Green glass orbs, glowing faintly with their own eldritch light, were suspended from the ceilings on bronze chains. Within them, Grïgnyr glimpsed distorted and horrifying shapes that briefly resolved themselves before disappearing.

All around him, laying on overstuffed pillows and the room's sumptuous carpet, were scantily-clad people collected in small groups and engaging in many different acts of pleasure. Most bore addled expressions of inebriation or of drug use, while a few others watched the hanging orbs, hooting and clapping at the strange vistas periodically revealed within.

A white marble dais arose in the center of the room. Upon it stood a golden chair, padded with thick, ruby-colored cushions. A short, broad-shouldered man, who might have once been powerfully-built, but who had seemed to have descended into sloth and decadence, sat upon it, presiding over the debauchery spread out before him. The man's bulk strained at the velvet fabric of his turquoise robes, and a silver diadem was set askew on his sweating forehead. He combed his thick, dark beard with his fingertips as the guards approached the dais, dragging Grïgnyr with them.

"Kneel before Agaphim, Prince of Gorzom," said the captain, even as the guards who had conveyed him tried to force him to his knees.

"By Myrk's hoary beard, I will not!"

His cries of defiance were of no use. Two of the guards kicked Grïgnyr in the backs of his knees. He fell heavily forward onto the carpet, while the captain smirked and the man in the golden chair looked on in confusion.

Grïgnyr's shouts had stilled the festive air in the room. Those revelers that still had some manner of their wits about them turned to look at the strange scene that played out before them, eyes wide and blinking. Prince Agaphim looked on as well, his pupils so large that they devoured the colors of his irises. His eyelids fluttered open and shut a dozen times, and the prince made a heaving, grunting noise, as if he were struggling to speak.

It was then that a man, whip-thin and jackal-featured, ascended the dais from behind the prince, stalking up so that he stood just behind and to one side of the golden chair. His iron grey hair was slicked back against his uneven skull, and his eyes, situated deep beneath his furrowed brows, were gimlet bright. Grïgnyr saw the hunger in this man, the lust and the craving for power that even his sumptuous, sapphire robes and his ring-bedecked hands could not hide.

The thin man pressed his hands together, and that gesture drew Grïgnyr's eye to the amulet about the man's neck. It was blood red, set in gold, and featured the symbol of the lidded eye—identical to the one inlaid on the pommels of many of the guards' weaponry.

Here, thought Grïgnyr, *is the true master of Gorzom.*

"What is...the meaning...of this intrusion?" demanded Prince Agaphim. "Broig. Explain yourself!"

The captain, who Grïgnyr presumed was Broig, sketched a lazy bow before his prince, but his gaze was only ever directed at the face of the man beside the throne. "Sire, please forgive me. I know that you are ever at work on important affairs of state, but this outlander's crimes warrant your immediate attention. My men and I prevented him from assaulting a serving girl in one of Gorzom's finest inns, and we also found evidence upon his person that suggests that he planned to foment rebellion against you."

"Rebellion?" said the prince, blinking rapidly and trying to focus on Grïgnyr. "Against Gorzom? Against me? You are a fool, outlander! I am master of this mighty city, and my hold on it is unbreakable!"

Now Grïgnyr laughed a cruel laugh. "You might have been master of this city once, oh prince, but no more! I can see the man you once were, even though it is all but obscured beneath the haze of your soporifics and the lethargy of your corpulence. Indeed, I can believe that once you were a man like me, who would punish his enemies with flame and blade until none dared raise a hand against you.

"But you are that man no more! You live in squalor within a decaying palace, your most loyal counsellors addled by drink and drugs. Your control is an illusion; your rulership a lie!"

"Silence!" roared Prince Agaphim, and in his voice, Grïgnyr heard the notched and rusted steel that had once been the prince's well-honed will.

The prince sucked in his girth and tried to sit straighter upon his golden chair. He blinked again, and Grïgnyr saw a sliver of color return to the man's eyes. "You dare to mock me in my own audience chamber? I, who am prince of Gorzom and the desert wastes beyond? By Sargoth, I shall see you flogged and broken for your insolence! Broig, show me the evidence of this man's cruelty and betrayal."

From within his tunic, Broig took out the leather pouch that had been, until recently, strapped to Grïgnyr's thigh. The guard captain, seemingly amused at his prince's sudden squall of wrath and pretentions of sobriety, favored the man behind the throne with an oily smile and lifted the pouch for his inspection.

"As you can see," said Broig, "within this pouch, this outlander carried the means to conquer not only Gorzom, but also the world entire. Yea, even to the gates of great Norgolia in the north."

"What do you mean?" said the prince, reaching out his hand. "You speak in portents and riddles. How could the contents of this small bag bring such devastation to Gorzom? Give it here and we will see the truth of your words."

But the man behind the throne neatly intercepted Prince Agaphim's grasping hand, taking the pouch from Broig and retreating with it behind the golden chair. Once there, the man opened the pouch and gazed within it, and the sight of the Eye tucked within its folds caused his face to adopt a most avaricious and terrifying expression.

"Agfand," said the prince, half-turning in his seat. "What is the meaning of this? What is in the pouch?"

Agfand stared down at the prince, his thin smile growing steadily wider as the brief surge of vitality that had animated Agaphim's form swiftly left it. Myrk's unconquerable frost spread across Grïgnyr's heart as the prince sagged heavily in his chair. In a moment, all concern, all anger, had faded from the man's countenance, leaving him again an empty vessel.

"My prince," said Agfand. "What Broig says is true. The contents of this pouch could make the one who held it the master of Gorzom and all the lands beyond. It is good, indeed, that your loyal guards have apprehended this outlander before he could carry out his intrigues against you."

"Good," said the prince, his voice thick and drowsy. "Very good."

"I could have the man flogged, as per your last command, or even sent to one of your many mines, that he might serve you until the cramped and dark spaces break his body…"

Prince Agaphim blinked, bleary-eyed. "Yes. That is wise. Glory to Gorzom and Sargoth."

"Or," said Agfand, "we could place him in the vaults, that he might entertain you and your…honored guests for so long as the blood continues to flow in his veins."

The prince's voice came out slow and faded, as if he were falling asleep. "Yes. A fitting end. Yes."

Agfand favored Grïgnyr with a reptilian smile. "Guardsmen, you have heard your sire's command. Throw the outlander…"

Grïgnyr surged forward, pitting all his strength against his captors. The two men that held him, exhausted by their long journey to the palace and no longer vigilant thanks to the strange scene playing out in the audience chamber, stumbled forward and fell upon the carpet as Grïgnyr wrenched free of their grasp. Someone in the assembly screamed, and Broig drew the Ecordian's stolen blade as Grïgnyr mounted the dais in a single bound.

Grïgnyr hands flew to the slender throat of Agfand, the corrupt counsellor, the poison at the heart of the city. He throttled the man as his momentum carried them both forward, such that Agfand soon lay sprawled upon the dais with Grïgnyr's full and savage weight atop him. The Ecordian felt the delicate bones in Agfand's throat creak and begin to give way as the prince's treacherous advisor clawed futilely at his mighty arms and gasped out an unintelligible curse.

At the same moment Agfand's neck collapsed with a brutal crunch, one of Broig's guardsmen brought the haft of his axe heavily down on the base of Grïgnyr's skull. Grïgnyr slumped to one side, crashing heavily into the prince's golden chair, and darkness claimed him for a second time that evening.

IV: THE VAULTS

AS HIS CONSCIOUSNESS RETURNED, Grïgnyr became aware of numerous bruises and abrasions on his limbs, which throbbed in angry time with his slowly-beating heart. He attempted to raise his head, but found that doing so brought such an intense wave of nausea that he vomited bile across the chilly floor.

Gingerly, Grïgnyr raised himself to a sitting position, resting his aching head against the cold, rough wall behind him. He feared, vaguely, that the repeated blows to his skull had struck him blind, for there was darkness all around him whether his eyes were opened or closed. To test this, he squeezed his eyelids shut and gently pressed upon them until flickering sparks danced across his vision. His eyes still lived, and for that, Grïgnyr whispered a prayer to Myrk.

Wherever he was, it was as dark as a tomb, and equally as cold. He wished for even the merest taper to see by.

He did not know how long he sat there before he felt himself recovered enough to rise to his feet. Grïgnyr held one hand over his head, lest he deal himself another blow against a low ceiling or other obstacle. His rise was unobstructed, however, and it seemed that whatever ceiling pressed down upon this cold and quiet place was well beyond the reach of his outstretched arm.

Keeping one hand on the wall to his left and the other thrust out before him, Grïgnyr walked. He advanced slowly, keeping all his weight on his back leg and sweeping the area before him with the pointed toe of his front foot. This allowed him to check to see if the floor before him had dropped off into a pit, or been blocked by a wall or other barrier, before he committed his full weight. In this methodical way, the Ecordian made his way through his new, stygian world.

Grïgnyr did not know how long he had progressed in this manner until the wall beside him abruptly ended. Feeling around, he discovered that the passage he had been following opened out into another, larger space of a size he could not easily determine by feel.

Grïgnyr stood there in the darkness, his hand seeking the stability of the wall that had been his constant guide and companion since his awakening, wondering what to do next. Should he retrace his steps and gain a more intimate understanding of his immediate environment? Should he venture off into the larger space, leaving the safety of the wall behind and possibly finding an escape from this chill and tenebrous place?

As he considered his options, his thoughts trickling slowly through his addled and injured brain, Grïgnyr slowly realized something.

He could see.

He could not see very much, but his eyes, now well-adjusted to the darkness of Prince Agaphim's vaults, were able to pick out the darker shadows of the walls and ceiling against the almost imperceptibly lighter areas of cold, still air that filled the room before him. Though his sight was keen from long years of nightly raiding and many escapades of nocturnal thievery, Grïgnyr knew even he would not have been able to discern corners and edges, walls and floors, without some sort of dimly glistering light.

And that light, he realized, must be ahead of him.

Grïgnyr took his hand off the wall and strode across the room before him, hoping that the path he took would bring him nearer, ever nearer, to that distant source of light. He soon discovered that he had chosen correctly, for the walls of his labyrinthine prison soon resolved out of the darkness, pale like naked bone in the growing radiance. At last, he turned a corner where, squinting against the sudden brightness, he beheld a room with as many hallways leading away from it as a wheel had spokes. Hanging on a chain from the vaulted ceiling was the source of the light—a green glass sphere that generated its own radiance without oil or tinder.

Grïgnyr stepped beneath the lamp, soaking in its emerald radiance, and found himself loathe to step away from it. The darkness beyond had weighed more heavily upon him than he had realized and, now that he was able to see both himself and his surroundings, he did not see any real need to throw himself back into its benighted depths.

As he stood there, bathing in the light, he noted certain similarities between this orb and the ones strung up about Prince Agaphim's audience chamber. Indeed, the only difference between the orbs was that this one lacked any distorted images or shadows flickering in its depths. Realizing this, Grïgnyr peered more closely, and noted that despite the smooth and reflective surface of the orb, it showed neither him, nor the room in which he stood, nor the thin, metal housing that held the orb suspended.

"I understand your fell sorceries now, Agfand!" said Grïgnyr, his voice echoing loudly in the room. "These are eyes as well as lamps! Like moths we are guided to their flame, so that you might see us and watch our suffering. By Myrk, I am glad that I have made your eyes go dark, so that you can no longer see or inflict suffering upon the people of Gorzom. And know you this, I shall soon win free of your city, once I leave this pit.

"To your prince, I say only this: Do you know now that your trusted vizier was also your jailer? Do you know that you have long been lord of this city in name only, trapped in a cage of stupor and excess while Agfand mocked you and held the key to your confinement? Whether the man you once were regains his mastery over yourself and your city, I care not, for I will take what is mine and left you and your city far behind me. So swears Grïgnyr the Ecordian!"

He had not expected an answer, but, in the distance, somewhere far beyond the range of the green light, a piercing, terrified cry split the darkness. Grïgnyr felt the old fire kindle in his blood and, heedless of his injuries and of the blackness spreading out infinitely before him, raced off to render aid.

*

The screams continued, now accompanied by staccato clattering sounds and by loud hissing noises that suggested to Grïgnyr some manner of large serpent. His keen senses, well-honed from a youth in the forests of Ecordia, allowed him to track the sounds with ease, and he drew closer to them with every step.

He was aided in his journey by the seeing orbs, which he now found hung at regular intervals in the various galleries and passageways he traversed. Their green light also revealed to Grïgnyr piles of bones and cloth that marked the final resting places of nameless souls condemned to the vaults before him. He paused only long enough to grab a sturdy femur from one collection of remains, offering up thanks to both Myrk and the bone's former owner as he continued onward toward the source of the noise.

He bounded around a corner and beheld such a sight that it brought him immediately to a halt. For there, bathed in the flameless light of another orb, two huge rats—larger than even the hardiest Ecordian mastiffs, hissed and drooled and circled around a slip of a woman clad in tattered clothing. Though the woman screamed, and though blood oozed from several lacerations upon her arms and cheek, she had planted her feet in a warrior's stance and kept the rats at bay with wild swings of a burning brand. Even now, the oily stench of burned fur assaulted Grïgnyr's nostrils, indicating that the woman had given as much injury as she had received.

With a wild shout, Grïgnyr threw himself on the back of the nearest rat. He slung the femur down beneath the beast's lower jaw and pulled upward on either end of it with both hands. The rat snarled and gnashed at him, but was unable to do more than spray him with its putrid spittle as Grïgnyr hoisted it off the ground and dragged it away from the woman.

"Grïgnyr!" the woman shouted, her eyes wide.

In the light of the burning brand, in the light of the seeing orb, he saw that her hair was the color of pale orchids. It was the woman from the inn— Carthena. Her mouth started to turn upward into a relieved smile before dropping into an O of horror.

"Look out!"

The other rat coiled and sprang at the Ecordian's, colliding full force with his mighty frame. The shock of the impact caused Grïgnyr's hands to jerk upward, snapping the dusty femur in two and inadvertently releasing the half-strangled body of the first rat. Grïgnyr toppled to one side, shuddering and howling as the second rat clawed its way up his side and sought to affix its diseased teeth in his shoulder.

Carthena leapt up beside him and began laying about the giant rat's head with the burning brand. The rat let out an inhuman shriek and whipped its charred muzzle around to bite at its new attacker. Grïgnyr took that moment to thrust upward with one of the halves of the broken femur, driving the jagged shard into a vulnerable spot just behind the rat's lower jaw. The rat screamed and thrashed in a death spasm, spraying Grïgnyr with its black and acrid blood.

As Grïgnyr kicked the rat's thrashing body off his own, he heard Carthena let out an ear-curdling shriek. The first rat, which had recovered somewhat from its strangulation, had attempted to clamp its filthy jaws around Carthena's calf. Though it had missed her flesh, the laces of her tall sandals had become entangled in the rat's fearsome teeth. The rat attempted to dislodge itself with a shake of its head, but was unable to do so, instead knocking Carthena off her feet.

Carthena fell, her torch rolling from her outstretched hands and down one of the numerous branching pathways. Her eyes were wide as she reached out for its retreating form, screaming in terror at her attacker, and at losing her only weapon.

But though the rat sorely menaced her, it had, in its bestial rage, forgotten Grïgnyr. Nor did it, with its maw entangled in the woman's lacings girl, have any way of defending itself. It died, surprised, when Grïgnyr thrust the other shard of broken femur through its eye and into its brain. The rat's mouth clattered open and shut as it died, allowing Carthena to pull her leg free. Crawling across the floor away from the cooling corpse of the beast, she recovered her brand and held it aloft.

In the quiet moment at the end of the battle, Grïgnyr noticed that Carthena's torch was crudely made from another femur and a crown of tightly-tied and dusty rags. He was impressed with her ingenuity, as she had not only thought to make a torch out of the remains of the dead, but also had been clever enough to find a way to ignite it.

Filled with awe at her cleverness and bravery, he arose, strode over to her, and offered her a hand. Carthena took it gratefully and arose to her feet. She took a moment to test the leg that had been worried by the giant rat and, finding that it was uninjured, gracefully put her weight upon it.

"You came at the nick of time, outlander," she said, pushing a curtain of tangled, orchid-colored hair away from her scratched face. "I am grateful for it."

"You seemed to be doing quite well before I came along," he replied. "Though I am pleased both to have rendered you aid and to see you again."

"Likewise," she said, after a long moment, gesturing down one of the dark hallways with her torch. "Let us take ourselves away from Agfand's watchful eyes, Ecordian. You and I have much to discuss."

"Aye, that we do," said Grïgnyr, "but you need no longer fear the Vizier of Gorzom, for I have crushed the life from him and sent him beyond the gates. Myrk even now passes judgment upon him."

Carthena cast a wary glance past him, up at the glowing orb chained to the ceiling. "Do not be so sure of your victory, Grïgnyr. There is much about Agfand, and about this city, that you do not know."

"That I can well believe," he said. "Lead on and I will hear all that you have to say."

*

They found a spot in a nearby tunnel that was out of view of the unblinking glass orb. Grïgnyr grunted as he sank down next to the cool stone wall, shifting his body as best as he could to ease his numerous injuries.

In the flickering light from the improvised torch, he saw that Carthena, though rattled and superficially wounded by the giant rats, seemed much haler and more alert than he.

"Agfand is a sorcerer," she said, "who usurped the throne of Gorzom from Agaphim using his fell magics. He gained his powers from a daemon god he serves, and he commands the undying loyalty of any in the city who bear the sigil of the lidded eye. His agents are everywhere, and his powers are very great. I cannot imagine that he would allow himself to be slain so easily, and I suspect that he has many proofs and wards on his person that protect him from harm."

Grïgnyr felt a trickle of fear trace an icy track down his spine. "What you say matches the evidence of mine own eyes. It was clear to me that the vizier ruled Gorzom. But, pray tell me, which of the powers does he serve?"

"Argol," said Carthena simply. "The very one whose Eye you bore out of Crin."

"So, as the legends hinted, it is no mere jewel."

Grïgnyr sank back against the smooth stone of the passage wall, overwhelmed by the revelation.

"Damn, and now the monster himself has it in his possession."

Carthena nodded. "You were a marked man long before you ever caught sight of Gorzom, The Sultana, much aggrieved at the loss of her treasure, sent messenger birds to all corners of the desert. Though she hated to do it, she told the leaders of the other nations of both your identity and the identity of that which you had taken. She promised a rich reward to any who would deliver both the Eye and your head to her in the Grand Palace of Crin.

"I should have been braver," she said, "and confronted you before you entered Gorzom, but I feared both your initial reaction and that other forces might be lying in wait outside the gates, so I waited until I could have discourse with you in a more private place. By then, it was too late."

She hung her head, but Grïgnyr shook his.

"Do not blame yourself," he said. "You are no oracle, though I am a little sorrowful that you did not seek to bring me warning solely for altruistic reasons."

Her laugh was hard and dry. "I would not risk myself for something so trivial as the life of an outlander," she said, her eyes darting down to the floor, "at least, I would not have before.

"But now what shall we do? The cult of Argol has both the Eye and control of Gorzom, and I suspect that they shall use it to restore Agfand and curry greater power and favor from their daemonic master."

"There is but one thing we can do," said Grïgnyr. "We must find the man and slay him, if he lives again, reclaiming the Eye that is mine by right of strength and low cunning, thus preventing the cult from using its power to extend its influence beyond Gorzom. I pray I live long enough to see the look on the wretch's face as I send him permanently beyond Myrk's grim gates.

"But to do that, we must first acquire weaponry and escape this labyrinth. I can do the first easily, but I fear it will take me too long to do the second."

Carthena uncoiled herself from her seat, a look of determination on her face. "With the second, I can help you. I know much of the vault's passageways and chambers, and I can, with some luck, lead you safely from here. Indeed, I was hoping to make my escape when I was beset upon by the rats."

Grïgnyr felt the weight on his heart grow lighter. "That is good. Very good. Give me a few moments to craft weapons for ourselves, so that we might defend ourselves against Agfand's beasts and cultists. Then, you and I shall find the exit and consider our next action from there."

Grïgnyr saw a flicker of something that might have been relief briefly appear in Carthena's eyes. "I will, but where will you find weapons down here?"

"Follow me." Grïgnyr favored her with a grim smile. "I will show you."

V: OUT OF THE DARKNESS

GRÏGNYR RETRACED HIS STEPS back to the chamber where the giant rats lay dead in congealing puddles of their own blood. Seizing one by the haunches, he dragged it back into the darkness of the passageway, glaring at the glowing orb all the while.

Once he was out of sight of the vizier's noxious eye, he withdrew the broken femur from the rat's corpse and scraped its jagged edge against the corridor wall. When the bone was as sharp as he could make it, he began slicing apart the rat's cheeks, parting skin, muscle, and sinew, slowly revealing the bone beneath. Carthena stood over him, illuminating his labors as best as she could with her dying torch.

"Tell me of this Sargoth," said Grïgnyr, as he continued scraping skin and flesh from the great rat's jaw.

"He is a god of mercy, of justice, of death by clean steel," she said, after a moment's silence. "I think that even one such as yourself would find reason to respect him, Grïgnyr."

"Indeed," he replied. "He sounds like a worthy god, and Myrk would likely drink and sup with him. Is his sigil that of the open hand?"

"It is. He came to the city with Agaphim, many years ago, aiding him in the usurpation of Argol's dreaded cult, which once ruled Gorzom and enslaved its people. In Sargoth's name, Agaphim routed them, smashing their altars with fire and sword.

Any that bore the lidded eye, he executed in the grand square before the palace. When, at last, he took the coronet and the throne, his first decree was that no one would ever again use the symbol of the lidded eye or speak Argol's name again."

By the guttering light of Carthena's torch, Grïgnyr continued his work, revealing more and more of the giant rat's lifeless jawbone. He thought on her words and said, "and yet now Argol's worshippers bear their sigils openly, and Agaphim does not raise his hand against them."

"This was all Agfand's doing," said she. "He presented himself as a benign figure, an advisor that would help our outlander prince rule the city he had so recently conquered. Once he had wormed himself into Agaphim's graces, he began weakening the prince's resolve with poisons and dark magic, until he became a shell of his former self. Now the once pristine shrines to Sargoth stand empty, and the lidded eye is open once again."

Grïgnyr set down his now blunted tool, flexed his hands, and, bending all his might to the prodigious task before him, tore the denuded lower jaw of the rat from its mouth. This he easily snapped into two gory pieces. He kept the right jawbone for himself and handed the left to Carthena. She took it dubiously, and her lip quivered in disgust.

"These are our weapons?" she asked.

"Aye," he said. "Take it by the slender part, above the tooth, and you may swing it as a cudgel to dangerous effect. Or, grip it by the place where it was once affixed to the skull and lash out, striking as quick as a serpent with the tooth. The teeth of normal rats are as strong as iron, and I suspect the teeth of their giant brethren are stronger still. These weapons will serve us very well until we can acquire blades of bronze and steel."

He arose, brushing away the bits of skin and fur that clung to him, and took up his half of the jaw-bone in a ready hand. "Now, Carthena, guide us out of this dreary tomb."

Carthena took up the right jawbone by the slender part, as instructed, and, with torch held high, led the pair through the tenebrous vaults of Gorzom.

*

They traveled on in silence, Carthena squinting at passageways and considering each of the small rooms they encountered. Sometimes, they walked for long stretches with little hesitation on her part. Other times, she spent what seemed an age deliberating which path to take, halting or doubling back upon seeing some feature noticeable only to herself.

"How is it," said Grïgnyr at last, "that you know so much of this labyrinth?"

For a long moment, she did not reply, but then she said, "I am the daughter of Minkardos, who is prince of Barwego. Our lands border Gorzom's on the northwest. Long had my father warred with the cult and its thralls, and joyful was he when, at long last, Agaphim threw down Argol's sigil and freed

Gorzom. So grateful was my father that he promised my hand to Agaphim, so that I might become Princess of Gorzom and unite our two lands in peace.

"Alas, upon my arrival in Gorzom, I discovered that my betrothed was an all but mindless husk, enslaved to his vizier's vile sorceries. Agfand soon had me imprisoned in a secret room within the palace. There, he wed me to my insensate husband in a mock ceremony, laughing all the while. As far as my father knows, I am happily married to his strongest ally, and he sees no need to suspect the denizens of the city that is now sister to Barwego."

She paused, and Grïgnyr watched her bring up the hand that held the jawbone, so that she could wipe her damp eyes upon her wrist.

"I was then plied with sorcery and drugs so that I would be yet one more of the legion of torpid hangers-on that attend upon the prince in his throne room. Unbeknownst to Agfand, my deep hatred of him gave me the strength to fight off his binding spells. What drugs he tried to give me I hid about the palace or left so that others could indulge upon them.

"Feigning stupor, I watched as the palace guards, most of whom were by now of the cult, brought the querulous and the criminal before the prince for judgment. Truly, however, all sentences were pronounced by Agfand, and every one of the convicted were borne away by the guard and tossed into the vaults. I watched their progress through this place on the seeing orbs hanging above the throne room, sending silent prayers to safeguard their souls."

Carthena's voice broke, and she gave a little sigh. Grïgnyr was about to approach her, to lay a reassuring hand on her shoulder, when she straightened her back and took a deep breath.

"It did not help. Most died down here, starving or butchered by strange beasts. The few that did escape, though promised full pardon and freedom, were swiftly pursued and slain by the guards. And yet, one good thing came of it—the longer I watched, the more I learned how the vaults were arrayed and how one might navigate them."

Grïgnyr did not prompt her for more of her story and the pair walked on in silence for a while. After crossing through one of the small chambers—and out of the range of one of Agfand's hanging orbs—she resumed her tale.

"I was working up the courage to escape when one of the guards brought the Sultana's missive to Agfand. He sent word to all his cultists to prepare for your arrival. I, knowing that I must find and warn you should you come this way, disappeared into the vaults. Fortune was with me, and I encountered none of the beasts as I made my way to one of the exits. The guard I found beyond that door was distracted by my beauty and thought that he and I might have a little dalliance before he set his brethren on me."

Carthena's hand, which gripped the rat's jawbone, shook with fury. "He was not aware of whom he had encountered, and it took no effort at all for me to seize his knife and plunge it betwixt his ribs."

"He was a degenerate and a fool," said Grïgnyr, angry at the cruel fortunes that Carthena had endured. "Had he been made of better mettle, he would have seen how formidable you were. It is good that the flame of his worthless life has been extinguished."

"Indeed," she said, before gesturing with a torch at a small room just ahead. "A door beyond this room that leads to one of the guards' chambers."

Grïgnyr nodded and, stealthy as a mountain cat, he crept past Carthena and into the doorway of the chamber. He paused, staring warily at the glowing orb hanging from the ceiling, wondering if anyone was watching them at that moment, wondering how many might be alert and ready for his presence on the other side of the heavy, wooden door.

"Myrk, let me live long enough to take my revenge."

No sooner was the whispered prayer gone from his lips that Grïgnyr sprang, racing across the chamber to throw his full weight against the portal on the far side. The door crashed inward, latch and hinges shattering from the force of his charge. Behind him, Carthena let out a string of oaths as he dropped into a fighting stance and surveyed the room around him.

A table stood in the middle of the room, upon it rested a green glass orb, similar in size and shape to the ones in the vaults and the prince's audience chamber. Within its glowing depths, a distorted

Carthena ran, waving torch and jawbone, ready to defend a hulking warrior who could be made out in a room just beyond.

Two of the palace guard had been, until moments before, seated at the table. Toppled chairs and scattered dice revealed the speed at which they had arisen, hands seeking weapons. They blinked in swollen-eyed terror at Grïgnyr, screamed at one another in panicked gibberish.

Grïgnyr took a two-handed grip upon the weightier end of his jawbone and stabbed, aiming the curved incisor of the dead rat at the nearest of the guards. The guard, his blade only half-drawn from his scabbard, was unable to avoid the attack. Grïgnyr let out a satisfied grunt as the rat tooth, empowered by his mighty thews, penetrated uniform and mail hauberk, sinking deeply into the tender flesh beneath. The guard let out a strangled gasp, and blood foamed from the corners of his mouth. He reeled away from Grïgnyr, clutched uselessly at the ragged hole in his chest, and collapsed.

The other guard, who had pulled his double-bitted axe free from the loop on his belt, rushed to the defense of his dying comrade. Grïgnyr ducked. The deadly axe swept over his head, slicing away a lock of his fiery red hair, but otherwise causing him no injury. Grïgnyr coiled for a spring, aiming the bloodied rat jaw at the abdomen of his new opponent.

Before he could make the leap, Carthena stepped up behind the guard and, with a savage cry, brought the weighty end of her jawbone down upon the man's unprotected head. The force of the blow deformed the guard's skull. The axe dropped from his nerveless hand and he fell, limp and lifeless, onto the floor beside it.

Grïgnyr set about the grim business of looting the guard's bodies for their armor and equipment. He had to all but untie the lacings on a cuirass so that it might fit over his well-muscled frame, and he discovered, to his dismay, that he could not put on either pair of the guards' armguards or leg greaves. He did, however, take up the fallen axe from the second guard, hefting its weight and giving it a few practice swings.

Carthena, for her part, did not avail herself of any of the guards' armor, though she did trade her makeshift brand for a much brighter resin torch ensconced in an iron bracket on the chamber's wall. She also laid her half of the rat's jawbone down beside Grïgnyr's, replacing it with a slender, well-balanced knife sheathed in the first guard's belt.

"Well done," said Grïgnyr. "We are free of that accursed place."

"Yes," said Carthena, a touch ruefully. "Now we have only to contend with the palace, the city beyond it, and the numberless members of the cult who will no doubt bar our way."

Grïgnyr's laugh was grim, but not wholly without mirth. "Either Myrk will see us free, or he will honor us after we fall in glorious battle. Lead onward, Carthena. Let us show all Gorzom that we are not to be trifled with."

With a sardonic smile, Carthena opened the door on the far side of the chamber and, torch raised, stepped out into the lowest level of Gorzom's great palace.

VI: THE CEREMONY

UNLIKE THE ROOMS ABOVE, which had degenerated into a den of filth and iniquity thanks to Agfand's fell influence, the subterranean chambers of the palace seemed to have merely been abandoned. The lower palace was a silent, echoing place, veiled in shadow and cobweb. In the light of Carthena's upraised torch, Grïgnyr beheld an occasional piece of fine carving, object of art, or case filled with long-forgotten treasures—symbols of Gorzom's more illustrious past that had been forgotten thanks to the twin curses of drugs and sorcery.

It was here that Carthena's sense of direction began to waver, and she confessed that she knew the twists and turns of the accursed vaults far better than those of the palace above. Grïgnyr continued to trust her instincts and assured her that, so long as they continued to ascend where they could, they would soon find themselves both above ground and in more familiar regions.

They were just starting across another lonesome gallery, bedecked with dusty tapestries and ringing hollowly with their footfalls, when a noise from the balcony above caused them to retreat into the hallway from whence they had come. Grïgnyr bade Carthena go farther back, so that the light of her torch would not be visible to anyone looking down from above. She obeyed with all swiftness and, as the darkness enfolded him, Grïgnyr noticed several lantern lights appear upon the balcony.

These lanterns were borne by a long procession of figures, all identically-clad in red silken vestments, faces covered with matching, expressionless, scarlet wooden masks. Around their necks, each one bore a large medallion much like the one that had been worn by Gorzom's vizier, which bore the lidded eye of the dread god Argol.

The procession continued along the balcony, and Grïgnyr saw that six members of it, who marched in the center, carried between them a long board whose contents were covered with a red silken cloth.

It marched in slow reverence, lanterns swinging, strange prayers issuing from the square mouth holes of their masks, toward the top of the wide staircase that led into the gallery below. Grïgnyr watched them until they began to descend, then he crept back down the hallway until he had reached Carthena's side.

"Cultists," he said. "Doubtless engaged in some profane rite."

Though her dark complexion paled slightly at the ill news, Carthena's face bore an expression of resolve. "If we are to find the Eye, and stop their plot, we must follow them."

"Indeed," said Grïgnyr. We shall wait until they have gone on their way, and then we will hunt them to their lair. Best to douse that torch, my lady, for darkness will now serve us as a far better ally than light will."

Carthena crushed the resin torch against the wall, grinding it until the flame died in a plume of smoke and sparks. Then the two of them returned to the mouth of the passageway and, at as safe a distance as they could manage, pursued the procession's dwindling lantern light.

*

They followed the cultists on a circuitous path that led them back down into the depths beneath the palace and the city. They passed through a plain passageway of uncarved and moldering brick, toward a pair of ancient doors engraved with ravens, rivers, vultures, skulls, vipers, and other beasts known to have power over the underworld.

Beyond these doors, Grïgnyr beheld the huge chamber that was the final resting place of the princes and princesses of old Gorzom. The chamber itself was a dead cavern, its ceiling thick with jagged stone spires.

Standing in regular intervals were mausoleums erected to house the remains of the departed rulers of the city. Those nearest to the entry portals were small and squat, featuring no ornamentation other than the names of the interred, their carved letters belonging to languages long dead. Each subsequent mausoleum was more ornate than the last, becoming larger and more splendid as Grïgnyr and Carthena followed the cultists.

Ahead of them, the procession halted at one of the grandest of the mausoleums. The two cultists at its head stepped forward and, by means of a pair of great keys, unlocked and opened the sepulcher's doors. Grïgnyr ducked behind the nearest tomb, bidding Carthena to accompany him, and from here, he waited as the procession filed into the mausoleum.

Grïgnyr soon resumed the chase, praying Myrk that the rearmost cultists in the procession would neither close nor bar the mausoleum doors behind them. The hoary old god continued to show Grïgnyr his good favor, for the doors remained open, allowing him and Carthena to pass inside. Beyond lay not a burial chamber, as Grïgnyr had expected, but a staircase leading even deeper into the earth.

He and Carthena looked at one another, readied their weapons, and, for the final time, descended.

*

The cavern beneath was dank and fetid. Though the procession had brought with them almost as many lanterns as they had numbers, the combined light did almost nothing to alleviate the oppressive gloom hanging over the place.

The floor of the cavern, unlike the one above, was perilous and uneven, broken up by clusters of stalagmites and piles of loose rock. The cultists threaded a path through these obstacles, moving snake-like toward a dark, cyclopean mass that dominated the far side of the cavern.

Grïgnyr and Carthena hurried after them. Using the stalagmites and other debris to screen themselves from those that they pursued, the pair took a zigzag track across the cavern, until they at last arrived on the far side.

The cultists, who had reached the far side well ahead of them, had hung their lanterns upon iron hooks set into the walls and outcroppings of stone for the purpose, and were in the process of arraying themselves in a semicircle about a stone dais. Situated at the back of the dais, looming both over it and the gathered supplicants, was a statue of a great and terrible beast.

The statue appeared, to Grïgnyr, to be carved out of one unfathomably large piece of jade, into the rough shape of a coiled, slug-like creature, poised in mid-undulation and glistening with the cavern's moisture. It possessed a head, of sorts, bloated and misshapen, that bent low over the center of the dais. The head was almost covered by a giant, puckered maw ringed with rows and rows of inward-pointing fangs. Above this ghastly mouth was carved a small hole, about the size of a man's fist, whose hollow was darker even than the deepest shadows of the cave.

As Grïgnyr watched, the six who had marched in the middle of the procession ascended the dais. With great pomp and gravity, they brought the covered board to the dais' center and laid it down beneath the statue's sharply stooping head. The six gathered into a line behind the object, dropped to their knees, and began a prayer dirge that was swiftly taken up by the others assembled there.

Then, as one, the six on the dais drew six short, bronze blades and plunged them into six chests. Six fountains of heart's blood erupted to anoint the cloth-covered thing upon the dais.

Carthena, seeing this, nearly screamed aloud, but she pushed her face into Grïgnyr's shoulder, and was able to stifle her cries.

Though Grïgnyr was unmoved at the sight of the six cultists spilling their own blood, what happened next filled him with such primal fear and revulsion that he gripped the stalagmite before him and fought, with all his strength, to keep down his gorge. For the thing that lay beneath the blood-soaked cloth began to stir, twisting and shaking like one trapped in the wild throes of falling sickness. As the prayer of the assembled cultists reached an ecstatic crescendo, the thing that lay upon the board sat up, and the bloodied shroud fell away.

Beneath sat a naked Agfand, his throat still livid with the prints left by Grïgnyr's hands. The vizier twisted his lips in a gruesome death rictus and raised his arms in benediction as the assembled cultists shrieked and cheered at his vile resurrection.

In one of Agfand's hands, Grïgnyr saw the vizier held a green jewel—The Eye of Argol.

Agfand slowly arose, wrapping the bloodied cloth loosely about him so that it served as a kind of makeshift vestment.

"My friends!" said Agfand, his voice hoarse. "Today is a most auspicious day! Thanks to the greed of the Sultana of Crin, thanks to the bumbling of an oaf from Ecordia, we have at last reclaimed that which is ours by right, stolen from our forebearers by heretics and apostates.

"Behold, my friends, the eye of our great and eternal god! No longer shall he writhe in blind slumber, unable to convey his will to us, unable to teach us the deepest lore of the Black Beyond! We stand, you and I, on the eve of his regeneration! No more will we have to skulk in shadows, doing his work in secret, manipulating prince and people by slow degrees and with painful intrigues. For Argol's restoration, long denied to him, is at long last at hand! With it, our power shall grow a thousand-fold, such that neither prince nor god shall stand against us! The soldiers of Crin, the mercenaries of Barwego, the legions of Norgolia will fall before our onslaught, helpless as we baptize the lands with the blood of the craven and the unrighteous!"

The cultists assembled around the dais had worked themselves into a berserk frenzy. They tore at their sacramental robes, clutched at the air with claw-like hands, and shrieked the names Agfand and Argol until the cavern fairly resounded with the awful syllables. As the ecstasy of the cultists reached its zenith, Agfand turned, took the Eye in both his hands, and lifted it toward the statue above him.

Carthena grasped at Grïgnyr's arm, "No, you fool! There are too many!"

But Grïgnyr was already racing across the cavern toward the profane altar, his blood pumping hot within his veins. A moment later, he threw himself on the backs of the rearmost of the cultists, hewing away at them with his axe.

He struck down five of the degenerate supplicants in as many seconds, but the rest, spurred to madness by their own zeal and by Agfand's fervor, closed in tightly around him, plucking daggers and short blades from the depths of their robes. In a moment, Grïgnyr was hemmed in on all sides, bleeding from a dozen cuts and lacerations. He lashed out at the masked horde with looping swings of his deadly axe, hewing down foe after foe, but it was not enough. Swiftly overcome by his own wounds, and by the weight of the cultists' numbers, Grïgnyr found himself driven to his knees, his arms wrenched painfully around behind his back. He let out one final grunt of defiance as the axe, which the cultists had wrung from his hand, clattered to the ground in a grim tintinnabulation.

His great strength and weight proved to be no match for the many hands that had been laid upon him and, in but a few moments, Grïgnyr had been heaved up onto the dais and into Agfand's presence. The vizier of Gorzom patted Grïgnyr's face with a hand sticky with sacrificial blood, grinning all the while.

"Ah, outlander," said Agfand. "I was sure that the vaults would have given you an ending fittingly brutal, but you have proven to be stronger and more cunning than I had expected."

Agfand held out the dully-glittering green jewel as if for Grïgnyr's approval or blessing. "It matters not. Indeed, I am glad that you are here, for who better to witness Argol's awakening and briefly slake his endless hunger than the fool of an outlander who brought his Eye out of Crin?"

Laughing, Agfand turned and, with both hands, again raised the Eye toward the head of that hideous statue. The revived vizier strained upward onto the tips of his toes, his entire body shaking as he struggled to seat the fist-sized emerald into the dark socket above the statue's mouth. A moment later, the jewel sank home with a wet, fleshy noise, and it began to glow with a fearsome light reminiscent of the globes that illuminated Gorzom's vaults.

The cavern shuddered, as if wracked by an earthquake, and the great dais beneath Grïgnyr's feet cracked and split apart. Above him, the sinusoidal statue of awful, wet stone, began to move, sloughing off the mud and filth of centuries as it lifted its great head over Grïgnyr and the cultists. The god's lesser devotees let out ecstatic cries as globules of black earth rained down upon them, staining their faces and blotching their red robes. Even Agfand was not unmoved by the sight, and he raised both head and hands to the terrible worm in welcoming supplication.

Grïgnyr struggled against the cultists, but he found he had not the strength to free himself from their combined grip. All he could do was look up helplessly as the daemon god rippled and undulated above him, its many rings of quill-like teeth rasping in its throat. As it began to secrete thick, bubbling slime from pores around its mouth, its Eye glowed brighter and brighter, so that there were no shadows left to shroud the horrible sight from Grïgnyr's view. He prayed to Myrk that his death would be quick, and that Carthena would somehow escape the cultists' depredations as his green eyes became fixed upon the god's solitary, luminous orb.

Within the depths of Argol's Eye, Grïgnyr beheld terrors and wonders that his primitive brain had no words to describe. He gazed into a fathomless emerald abyss, populated with cavorting shapes that spun wildly in complicated patterns. Most of the time, these patterns held no meaning, but on occasion, one or several groups of shapes resolved themselves into something that looked not unlike a hieroglyph from a language long lost to the peoples of the world. These symbols remained only for an instant, and Grïgnyr was glad, for had they retained their shape for but a moment more, he might have understood their significance, and through them, gained frightening insights into the secrets of the universe.

The shapes gyrated at greater and greater speed, whirling and twirling through the endless green expanse. Grignr felt himself falling past them, heard them calling his name with susurrus voices. The emerald void darkened as he fell, and now Grïgnyr beheld loathsome beasts, slithering and gibbering just beyond the range of his vision. He knew, somehow, that it would not be long before the dimming light would fail completely. He knew that when it did, the beasts, under cover darkness, would come forth to devour him body and soul.

Grïgnyr screamed, for a jolt of bright, clean pain seared into his calf, making its way, at lightning speed, toward the numbed and ensorcelled portions of his brain. He came awake with a start as the sickly green world of Argol's Eye shattered to pieces and fell away around him. He found that he was trapped within the slimy coils of the daemon god's worm-like body, hoisted a dozen feet or more off the shattered dais. Above him was Argol's maw, opened wide and trembling as it prepared to devour its sacrifice. Below him, the surviving cultists, with eyes closed, swayed and chanted to their god. Behind them, a look of panic and hope on her face, stood Carthena.

"Grïgnyr! The Eye!" she cried. "Take the Eye!"

Shaking off the last of his trance, Grignr looked down and saw the hilt of a well-balanced knife protruding from the muscles of his calf.

How Carthena had known that pain would break Argol's fugue, he had no idea. That she had struck him with an almost impossible throw filled him with awe.

Sending prayers of thanks to hoary Myrk, to forgotten Sargoth, to wily Carthena, Grïgnyr pulled his arm free of Argol's fleshy coils and, with great effort, yanked the knife out of the wound in his leg. A freshet of his own blood spilled down onto the cultists below, but Grignr cared not about his injury. His whole being, body and soul, was bent to one purpose—stopping Argol.

With a furious cry, Grignr drove the knife into the gap between Eye and socket, forcing it to the hilt in Argol's worm-like head. The daemon god spasmed in agony, nearly pulverizing Grïgnyr in its coils, and let out a roar that all but deafened the Ecordian.

Gritting his teeth against the pain, Grïgnyr dug and twisted with his knife, working it down and behind the Eye. The creature roared again, and Grignr felt several of his ribs splinter in Argol's grip, but the dreadful, luminous Eye popped free with a sickening noise.

Grignr seized the emerald in both of his hands and, with all the strength that was left to him, hurled it down onto the floor of the cavern. Only a few of the cultists realized what had happened, and of these, only one or two had the presence of mind to try and intercept the Eye on its downward trajectory, but they were simply not fast enough. Their hands grasped at empty air as the Eye flashed past them, striking the cavern floor and shattering into a dozen jagged fragments.

Argol reeled back, as if it were about to hurl itself forward and dash both itself and Grignr into pieces upon the dais. Yet whatever motile power the daemon god possessed immediately deserted it when the Eye was destroyed. It froze in place in a tortured posture above the dais, Grignr held tightly in its now immobile coils. The final blow would never come.

The cultists, seeing their almighty god reduced permanently to insensate stone, turned and fled from the dais, weeping and shrieking. Last to go was Agfand and, though he did not give himself over to emotion like the others of the cult, he favored Grïgnyr and Carthena with a look of utter hatred as he ran for the steps that led back up into the palace crypts, gripping the bloodied shroud tightly about his gaunt frame.

Grïgnyr paid the cultists but little mind, as he was overcome by the agony of his wounds and the sorrow of losing so great a prize as the Eye of Argol. He hung there in the stone coils of the dead god until Carthena, with deft fingers and delicate step, managed to ascend Argol's worm-like body and, between the strength of her arm and the power of her words, was able to wrestle Grïgnyr free of his imprisonment.

A time later, the two of them lay resting upon the ruined dais, surrounded by dead cultists and overshadowed by a daemon that would remain a statue until the fall of the world.

"You are brave, my lady," said Grignr, breathing shallowly so as not to disturb his fractured ribs.

"You are a fool, outlander," said Carthena, though there was mirth and fondness in her voice.

Grignr gestured at the maw of dead Argol. "And between us, look what we have wrought."

"Indeed," she said, and commenced to laughing.

VII: THE LIBERATION OF GORZOM

GRÏGNYR, CLUTCHING HIS RIBS PROTECTIVELY with one arm, followed Carthena on a slow and winding track up out of the bowels of the palace. The way was easy enough, especially once they had mounted the stairs to the gallery upon which Grïgnyr had first espied the cultists' procession, and soon they had reached a level where they could see the first rays of the dawning sun shining over the shuttered houses of upper Gorzom.

As they climbed, they found the palace abuzz with activity, as if it was a hornets' nest stirred to action by a well-placed kick. The many courtiers and functionaries of the palace, seemingly awake for the first time in an age, wandered blearily around the corridors, greeting one another and trying to ascertain what day it was and why the palace apartments were in such disarray. Grïgnyr allowed himself a smirk when, upon passing by a doorway leading to one of Sargoth's shrines, he beheld two elderly servants of the palace clucking and fretting over the sorry state of the altar goods.

The few denizens that took note of Grïgnyr and Carthena raised an eyebrow or gawped at them strangely. However, these, like the others, were more concerned with what had happened to themselves than with the passage of two injured and exhausted people through the grand galleries and courtyards of the palace, and so let them go on with nary a word.

"It seems that Agfand's spell is well and truly broken," said Grïgnyr, once he and Carthena were alone again in a shady corner of the palace grounds. "By Myrk, I am pleased to see it."

"As am I," she replied. "Though he has escaped justice, it seems that the vizier and his daemonic power no longer plague the goodly people of Gorzom. I only pray that Prince Agaphim is also free of the curse of Argol, and that he, upon hearing of your heroics, will see fit to reward you for the prowess and courage you displayed in the defense of a people not your own."

Grïgnyr nodded and smiled, for he had assumed for some time now that Carthena, consciously or not, was winging her way to her betrothed by the most direct means she could manage. "Even if he cares not for me or my deeds, so long as he provides me with food and a place to rest while my wounds heal, I shall be grateful to him for the rest of my days."

With hearts thus uplifted, they proceeded at greater pace to the uppermost reaches of the palace, where Prince Agaphim's audience chamber and apartments were situated. Their ebullience did not last for very long for, as they reached the inner courtyard surrounding the prince's private quarters, they found its numerous inhabitants, now awake and with their wits about them, shouting warnings to one another and seeking out places to hide amongst the courtyard's overgrown greenery.

"You there," said Carthena, an edge of imperiousness to her voice that was not at all out of place with her handsome physique or her fine carriage. "What is the meaning of this commotion? What has happened?"

The man she addressed was sunken-eyed and scrawny, clad only in the ragged ruins of a linen chiton. He reeked of sweat and lotus oils, and his breath was noxious and unperfumed.

"Agfand, the prince's vizier!" said the man, pointing up to the tower where the audience chamber lay. "He seeks to slaughter Prince Agaphim and is accompanied by traitorous guardsmen loyal to his cause. Flee, my lady, flee, before he finds you and slays you, as well!"

With that, the man, his soul as yellow as his jaundiced skin, plunged into the overgrown trees in the center of the courtyard and was lost to sight.

Grïgnyr spared no more than a backward glance as he followed Carthena up the steps to the prince's apartments, gritting his teeth and grunting as his ribs creaked from the effort.

*

The many glass globes that had once illuminated the audience chamber now hung dark and powerless within their cages, able only to reflect the gruesome scene that played out in the room below.

The surviving cultists, many of whom were now unmasked, had smashed their way into the chamber scant moments before, breaking the thick wooden doors free from their hinges and dashing them to pieces upon the carpet. Those of the prince's inner court who remained within the chamber sought to defend themselves with bits of furniture, broken amphorae, or with whatever other objects that came easily to hand. Alas, they were weak from months of long indolence and stupor, and those that were not killed outright were swiftly disarmed.

Prince Agaphim gave a good accounting of himself, taking up his own regnal seat by the back and laying low two of the armed cultists with it. Alas, he was soon overwhelmed, and a sharp blow to his head sent him reeling into a pile of soiled pillows.

In the aftermath, Agfand seized the prince's chair, righted it, and seated himself upon its plush cushions.

"Though we have lost the power of Argol today," he intoned, "we are still the mightiest faction in all of Gorzom. To that end, my friends, I have decided to depose this weakling prince that I have manipulated for so long and rule this city as its true lord. Starting today, the symbol of the Eye shall be flown from every tower in Gorzom, and any who stand against it or me shall be put to a miserable death."

"Damn you, you wretch," gasped Agaphim. "I thought you were my friend and confidant, but now that your spell is broken, I see that you are nothing more than a scheming sorcerer and a traitor. Know that, even if I die here and now, your reign will not last until high sun! The righteous Gorzomi hate Argol and all he stands for, and they will rend you asunder and leave your broken corpse for the vultures."

"Brave words indeed, but hollow," said Agfand. To the amassed cultists, he said, "Broig?"

One of the still-masked cultists, who held a large and deadly broadsword in his hands, stepped forward, "Yes, my lord?"

"Kill the swine and bring me his head."

"With pleasure, my lord."

As Broig strode toward the prince to carry out his master's command, a battle cry resounded along the outer hallway. Agfand raised his head at the sound and beheld a giant of a man, pale-skinned and fire-haired, racing toward him, a gore-encrusted axe gripped in one hand. Behind him came the strumpet from Barwego, her orchid locks trailing behind her head like a battle standard. And though she gave no cry, when she looked upon Agfand, the glint in her eye betrayed her murderous intentions.

"No!" screamed Agfand. "Stop them!"

*

The agony of his injuries faded away as a familiar bloodlust took hold of Grïgnyr. Roaring a challenge to the vizier and his followers, he stormed through the ruined portal and into the audience chamber. With one blow of his axe, he severed the spine of the nearest cultist. With another, he shattered both a ritual mask and the skull of the Argolite beneath it. The remaining cultists fanned out and away from him, their weapons at the ready, while the innocents fled to the farthest corners of the room.

One of the cultists, who had until now been busily hauling Agaphim to Agfand's feet, let go of the of the prince and faced Grïgnyr.

Grïgnyr's eyes narrowed when he beheld the sword that the cultist held in his hands. Even before the man removed his mask and cast it to one side, that he might see better in the melee that was sure to follow, Grïgnyr knew that it was Broig.

"Outlander dog," snarled Broig. "I should have killed you when I had the chance."

"Had you done so, you and your master might have succeeded," said Grïgnyr.

"There is still time for that mistake to be rectified," shouted the other, as he bounded across the audience chamber toward Grïgnyr, sword raised.

Gritting his teeth to distract himself from the pain in his ribs, Grïgnyr gripped the handle of his axe in both hands and raised it above his head. With all his strength, he hurtled the weapon at Broig, who threw himself full length on the carpet to avoid the it.

The axe continued, tumbling in its deadly arc, until it sank with a meaty thud into Agfand's narrow chest. The force of the impact was so great that it threw Agfand's body against the back of the chair, toppling it, and him, over backward onto the floor.

Broig struggled to rise, that he might finish his desperate charge and skewer the Ecordian. He had just gotten to his hands and knees when Grignr leaped at him, kicking the captain full in the face with sandaled foot. Broig's nose shattered in a spray of blood and mucous, and he collapsed, sobbing and gurgling, upon the carpet.

In the silence that followed, Grïgnyr fetched up his broadsword, glad to feel the reassuring weight of it in his hand. He stared at the now sniveling cultists with a baleful eye, silently daring them to attack him. None of them did. A few fell in dead faints.

With a final swing of his sword, Grïgnyr ended Broig's life. Then, to the cultists, he said.

"Your god is dead. Your master is dead. You are finished. On your knees, worms!"

The cultists sank to the bloodied carpet, all fire and religious fervor gone from their quaking bodies. As they did so, the courtiers stepped forward, emboldened by Grïgnyr's display of prowess. Using what cords and cloths they had, they bound the cultists so that they could not escape.

By this time, Prince Agaphim, his face covered with a sheet of his own blood, had arisen from his prostrate position beside the toppled chair. He surveyed the aftermath of Grïgnyr's assault with a bemused and bewildered eye for a long moment before favoring the Ecordian with a nod.

"Who are you?" said the prince at last. "And who is the lady that comes with you?"

"I am Grïgnyr of Ecordia, a wanderer who happened upon your city and its many intrigues by accident. The lady is none other than Carthena of Barwego, daughter to the duke of that place, and your betrothed. She has spared no effort in her attempts to free you from Agfand's machinations and restore you to your rightful place upon the throne of Gorzom."

Upon hearing these words, Prince Agaphim adopted an expression of contrition and shame. He daubed at his bloody face with his sleeve and bowed slightly, unable to meet Carthena's eye.

"Great lady, I am honored to at last receive you, even if I must do so in such a state."

"I am glad to meet you at last, my betrothed," said Carthena, with a graceful curtsey. "I care not about the state of your person or of your city, so long as you are once again of sound mind."

"It appears that I am, at that," said the prince, "and it appears that I have you and the Ecordian to thank for it.

"I must confess that I am like a man who has awakened from a long and troubled sleep, and I am not aware of what has transpired in my dotage. Give me a moment to summon the portion of my soldiers that are still loyal to me, that I might begin the great effort of purging my city of Argol and his evil eye. Then you and I shall sit and sup, and you shall tell me your no doubt unbelievable and harrowing tale."

Grïgnyr nodded sharply, once. "It shall be my honor to do so, oh prince."

*

And so, it came to pass that Grïgnyr convalesced in pampered comfort as an honored guest of Prince

Agaphim of Gorzom, and it was not very long at all before his wounds had healed and he was as hale and as strong as he had ever been.

Soon growing bored with the ease of palace life, Grïgnyr took to exercising daily in the palace court-yards, and so prodigious were his feats of strength and martial prowess that the prince himself swiftly joined him in his exertions. It was soon a daily occurrence that the two men sparred and practiced in the open air together, and all who saw them remarked on the prince's improved countenance, physique, and vigor.

In time, those forces within the city who were loyal to Prince Agaphim routed out the last of the cultists of Argol, destroying their icons, altars, and paraphernalia, and placing their heads on pikes arrayed around the city walls. Once the darkness had, at last, been expunged from Gorzom, the prince re-consecrated the altars and shrines of Sargoth within the city and announced a week-long feast of celebration and thanksgiving. At the end of the week, at the height of the celebration, in solemn ceremony, Prince Agaphim wed Carthena of Barwego, at last making her Princess of Gorzom and sealing a lasting alliance with her father, the duke.

Grïgnyr had but little to his name, apart from his sword, the few clothes graciously given to him by the prince and princess, and the three Simarian horses that had, until now, been stabled and lavishly cared for near the city gates. Two of these noble steeds he gave to Agaphim and Carthena as a wedding present, but the last he kept for himself, weighing down the beast with such weaponry and supplies as he could easily transport.

"We are sorry to see you go," said Agaphim who had, with Carthena, come all the way to the outskirts of the city in the early morning to see Grïgnyr off. "You have made yourself quite a legacy here in Gorzom. Why not stay, rest upon your laurels, and take as many titles and honors as we see fit to offer you?"

Grïgnyr smiled. "I am honored, oh prince, but I am not a man of civilization as you are. Gorzom becomes smaller and smaller to me with each passing day, and I can feel an itching in my feet and a stirring in my blood which spurs me ever onward, seeking new lands and new adventures."

"We understand," said Carthena, smiling up at the mighty Ecordian. "Know that if your journeys ever bring you here again, or to the gates of my father's house in Barwego, you will find shelter, safety, and friendship for as long as you may require it."

Grïgnyr bowed solemnly. "I am most grateful for your thanks, oh princess. I know that your cunning and deadly grace will be a better safeguard to Gorzom and its prince than any phalanx of mercenaries or cabal of dreadful magicians."

With that, he embraced his friends, mounted up upon his steed, and rode out of Gorzom's western gates, the light of the rising sun shining brightly behind him.

THE END

THE EYE OF ARGON

By Jim Theis

What follows is the original version of the story, written in 1970 by Jim Theis. It is preserved here for posterity. All spellings, grammatical mistakes, punctuation errors, layout errors, and similar, have been preserved to the best of my ability.

I have assumed, based on the vast circulation of this work, and the fact that it has been reprinted by at least two publishers, that The Eye of Argon *has fallen into the public domain.*

If this is inaccurate, please let me know, and I will happily remove this section from future editions of this work.

—   Geoff Bottone

-1-

THE WEATHER BEATEN TRAIL WOUND AHEAD into the dust racked climes of the baren land which dominates large portions of the Norgolian empire. Age worn hoof prints smothered by the sifting sands of time shone dully against the dust splattered crust of earth. The tireless sun cast its parching rays of incandescense from overhead, half way through its daily revolution. Small rodents scampered about, occupying themselves in the daily accomplishments of their dismal lives. Dust sprayed over three heaving mounts in blinding clouds, while they bore the burdonsome cargoes of their struggling overseers.

"Prepare to embrace your creators in the stygian haunts of hell, barbarian", gasped the first soldier.

"Only after you have kissed the fleeting stead of death, wretch!" returned Grignr.

A sweeping blade of flashing steel riveted from the massive barbarians hide enameled shield as his rippling right arm thrust forth, sending a steel shod blade to the hilt into the soldiers vital organs. The disemboweled mercenary crumpled from his saddle and sank to the clouded sward, sprinkling the parched dust with crimson droplets of escaping life fluid.

The enthused barbarian swilveled about, his shock of fiery red hair tossing robustly in the humid air currents as he faced the attack of the defeated soldier's fellow in arms.

"Damn you,barbarian" Shrieked the soldier as he observed his comrade in death.

A gleaming scimitar smote a heavy blow against the renegade's spiked helmet, bringing a heavy cloud over the Ecordian's misting brain. Shaking off the effects of the pounding blow to his head, Grignr brought down his scarlet streaked edge against the soldier's crudely forged hauberk, clanging harmlessly to the left side of his opponent. The soldier's stead whinnied as he directed the horse back from the driving blade of the barbarian. Grignr leashed his mount forward as the hoarsely piercing battle cry of his wilderness bred race resounded from his grinding lungs. A twirling blade bounced harmlessly from the mighty thief's buckler as his rolling right arm cleft upward, sending a foot of blinding steel ripping through the Simarian's exposed gullet. A gasping gurgle from the soldier's writhing mouth as he tumbled to the golden sand at his feet, and wormed agonizingly in his death bed.

Grignr's emerald green orbs glared lustfully at the wallowing soldier strugg-ling before his chestnut swirled mount. His scowling voice reverberated over the dying form in a tone of mocking mirth. "You city bred dogs should learn not to antagonize your better." Reining his weary mount ahead, grignr resumed his journey to the Noregolian city of Gorzam, hoping to discover wine, women, and adventure to boil the wild blood coarsing through his savage veins.

The trek to Gorzom was forced upon Grignr when the soldiers of Crin were leashed upon him by a faithless concubine he had wooed. His scandalous activities throughout the Simarian city had unleashed throngs of havoc and uproar among it's refined patricians, leading them to tack a heavy reward over his head. He had barely managed to escape through the back entrance of the inn he had been guzzling in, as a squad of soldiers tounced upon him. After spilling a spout of blood from the leader of the mercenaries as he dismembered one of the officer's arms, he retreated to his mount to make his way towards Gorzom, rumoured to contain hoards of plunder, and many young wenches for any man who has the backbone to wrest them away.

-2-

ARRIVING AFTER DUSK IN GORZOM, grignr descended down a dismal alley, reining his horse before a beaten tavern. The redhaired giant strode into the dimly lit hostelry reeking of foul odors, and cheap wine. The air was heavy with chocking fumes spewing from smolderingtorches encased within theden's earthen packed walls. Tables were clustered with groups of drunken thieves, and cutthroats, tossing dice, or making love to willing prostitutes.

Eyeing a slender female crouched alone at a nearby bench, Grignr advanced wishing to wholesomely occupy his time. The flickering torches cast weird shafts of luminescence dancing over the half naked harlot of his choice, her stringy orchid twines of hair swaying gracefully over the lithe opaque nose, as she raised a half drained mug to her pale red lips.

Glancing upward, the alluring complexion noted the stalwart giant as he rapidly approached. A faint glimmer sparked from the pair of deep blue ovals of the amorous female as she motioned toward Grignr, enticing him to join her. The barbarian seated himself upon a stool at the wenches side, exposing his body, na ed save for a loin cloth brandishing a long steel broad sword, an iron spiraled battle helmet, and a thick leather sandals, to her unobstructed view.

" Thou hast need to occupy your time, barbarian",questioned the female?

"Only if something worth offering is within my reach." Stated Grignr,as his hands crept to embrace the tempting female, who welcomed them with open willingness.

"From where do you come barbarian, and by what are you called?" Gasped the complying wench, as Grignr smothered her lips with the blazing touch of his flaming mouth.

The engrossed titan ignored the queries of the inquisitive female, pulling her towards him and crushing her sagging nipples to his yearning chest. Without struggle she gave in, winding her soft arms around the harshly bronzedhide of Grignr corded shoulder blades, as his calloused hands caressed her firm protruding busts.

"You make love well wench,"Admitted Grignr as he reached for the vessel of p potent wine his charge had been quaffing.

A flying foot caught the mug Grignr had taken hold of, sending its blood red contents sloshing over a flickering crescent; leashing tongues of bright orange flame to the foot trodden floor.

"Remove yourself Sirrah, the wench belongs to me;" Blabbered a drunken soldier, too far consumed by the influences of his virile brew to take note of the xsuperior size of his adversary.

Grignr lithly bounded from the startled female, his face lit up to an ashen red ferocity, and eyes locked in a searing feral blaze toward the swaying soldier.

"To hell with you, braggard!" Bellowed the angered Ecordian, as he hefted his finely honed broad sword.

The staggering soldier clumsily reached towards the pommel of his dangling sword, but before his hands ever touched the oaken hilt a silvered flash was slicing the heavy air. The thews of the savages lashing right arm bulged from the glistening bronzed hide as his blade bit deeply into the soldiers neck, loping off the confused head of his senseless tormentor.

With a nauseating thud the severed oval toppled to the floor, as the segregated torso of Grignr's bovine antagonist swayed, then collapsed in a pool of swirled crimson.

In the confusion the soldier's fellows confronted Grignr with unsheathed cutlasses, directed toward the latters scowling make-up.

"The slut should have picked his quarry more carefully!" Roared the victor in a mocking baritone growl, as he wiped his dripping blade on the prostrate form, and returned it to its scabbard.

"The fool should have shown more prudence, however you shall rue your actions while rotting in the pits."Stated one of the sprawled soldier's comrades.

Grignr's hand began to remove his blade from its leather housing, but retarded the motion in face of the blades waving before his face.

"Dismiss your hand from the hilt, barbarbian, or you shall find a foot of steel sheathed in your gizzard."

Grignr weighed his position observing his plight, where-upon he took the soldier's advice as the only logical choice. To attempt to hack his way from his pre-sent predicament could only warrant certain death. He was of no mind to bring upon his own demise if an alternate path presented itself. The will to necessitate his life forced him to yield to the superior force in hopes of a moment of carelessness later upon the part of his captors in which he could effect a more plausible means of escape.

"You may steady your arms, I will go without a struggle."

"Your decision is a wise one, yet perhaps you would have been better off had you forced death," the soldier's mouth wrinkled to a sadistic grin of knowing mirth as he prodded his prisoner on with his sword point.

After an indiscriminate period of marching through slinking alleyways and dim moonlighted streets the procession confronted a massive seraglio. The palace area was surrounded by an iron grating, with a lush garden upon all sides.

The group was admitted through the gilded gateway and Grignr was ledalong a stone pathway bordered by plush vegitation lustfully enhanced by the moon's shimmering rays. Upon reaching the palace the group was granted entrance, and after several minutes of explanation, led through several winding corridors to a richly draped chamber.

Confronting the group was a short stocky man seated upona golden throne. Tapestries of richly draped regal blue silk covered all walls of the chamber, while the steps leading to the throne were plated with sparkling white ivory. The man upon the throne had a naked wench seated at each of his arms, and a trusted advisor seated in back of him. At each cornwr of the chamber a guard stood at attention, with upraised pikes supported in their hands, golden chainmail adorning their torso's and barred helmets emitting scarlet plumes enshrouding their heads. The man rose from his throne to the dias surrounding it. His plush turquois robe dangled loosely from his chunky frame.

The soldiers surrounding Grignr fell to their knees with heads bowed to the stone masonry of the floor in fearful dignity to their sovereign, leige.

"Explain the purpose of this intrusion upon my chateau!"

"Your sirenity, resplendent in noble grandeur, we have brought this yokel before you (the soldier gestured toward Grignr) for the redress or your all knowing wisdom in judgement regarding his fate."

"Down on your knees, lout, and pay proper homage to your sovereign!" commanded the pudgy noble of Grignr.

"By the surly beard of Mrifk, Grignr kneels to no man!" scowled the massive barbarian.

"You dare to deal this blasphemous act to me! You are indeed brave stranger, yet your valor smacks of foolishness."

"I find you to be the only fool, sitting upon your pompous throne, enhancing the rolling flabs of your belly in the midst of your elaborate luxuryand . . ."

The soldier standing at Grignr's side smote him heavily in the face with the flat of his sword, cutting short the harsh words and knocking his battered helmet to the masonry with an echo-ing clang.

The paunchy noble's sagging round face flushed suddenly pale, then pastily lit up to a lustrous cherry red radiance. His lips trembled with malicious rage, while emitting a muffled sibilant gibberish. His sagging flabs rolled like a tub of upset jelly, then compressed as he sucked in his gut in an attempt to conceal his softness.

The prince regained his statue, then spoke to the soldiers surrounding Grignr, his face conforming to an ugly expression of sadistic humor.

"Take this uncouth heathen to the vault of misery, and be sure that his agonies are long and drawn out before death can release him."

"As you wish sire, your command shall be heeded immediately," answered the soldier on the right of Grignr as he stared into the barbarians seemingly unaffected face.

The advisor seated in the back of the noble slowly rose and advanced to the side of his master, motioning the wenches seated at his sides to remove themselves. He lowered his head and whispered to the noble.

"Eminence, the punishment you have decreed will cause much misery to this scum, yet it will last only a short time, then release him to a land beyond the sufferings of the human body. Why not mellow him in one of the subterranean vaults for a few days, then send him to life labor in one of your buried mines. To one such as he, a life spent in the confinement of the stygian pits will be an infinitely more appropiate and lasting torture."

The noble cupped his drooping double chin in the folds of his briming palm, meditating for a moment upon the rationality of the councilor's word's, then raised his shaggy brown eyebrows and turned toward the advisor, eyes aglow.

". . .As always Agafnd, you speak with great wisdom. Your words ring of great knowledge concerning the nature of one such as he ," sayeth , the king. The noble turned toward the prisoner with a noticable shimmer reflecting in his froglike eyes, and his lips contorting to a greasy grin. "I have decided to void my previous decree. The prisoner shall be removed to one of the palaces underground vaults. There he shall stay until I have decided that he has sufficiently simmered, whereupon he is to be allowed to spend the remainder of his days at labor in one of my mines."

Upon hearing this, Grignr realized that his fate would be far less merciful than death to one such as he, who is used to roaming the countryside at will. A life of confinement would be more than his body and mind could stand up to. This type of life would be immeasurably worse than death.

"I shall never understand the ways if your twisted civilization. I simply defend my honor and am condemned to life confinement, by a pig who sits on his royal ass wooing whores, and knows nothing of the affairs of the land he imagines to rule!" Lectures Grignr ?

"Enough of this! Away with the slut before I loose my control!"

Seeing the peril of his position, Grignr searched for an opening. Crushing prudence to the sward, he plowed into the soldier at his left arm taking hold of his sword, and bounding to the dias supporting the prince before the startled guards could regain their composure. Agafnd leaped Grignr and his sire, but found a sword blade permeating the length of his ribs before he could loosed his weapon.

The councilor slumped to his knees as Grignr slid his crimsoned blade from Agfnd's rib cage. The fat prince stood undulating in insurmountable fear before the edge of the fiery maned comet, his flabs of jellied blubber pulsating to and fro in ripples of flowing terror.

"Where is your wisdom and power now, your magjesty?" Growled Grignr.

The prince went rigid as Grignr discerned him glazing over his shoulder. He swlived to note the cause of the noble's attention, raised his sword over his head, and prepared to leash a vicious downward cleft, but fell short as the haft of a steel rimed pike clashed against his unguarded skull. Then blackness and solitude. Silence enshrouding and ever peaceful reind supreme.

"Before me, sirrah! Before me as always! Ha, Ha Ha, Haaaa...", nobly cackled.

-3-

CONSCIOUSNESS RETURNED TO GRIGNR in stygmatic pools as his mind gradually cleared of the cobwebs cluttering its inner recesses, yet the stygian cloud of char -coal ebony remained. An incompatible shield of blackness, enhanced by the bleak abscense of sound.

Grignr's muddled brain reeled from the shock of the blow he had recieved to the base of his skull. The events leading to his predicament were slow to filter back to him. He dickered with the notion that he was dead and had descended or sunk, however it may be, to the shadowed land beyond the the aperature of the grave, but rejected this hypothesis when his memory sifted back within his grips. This was not the land of the dead, it was something infinitely more precarious than anything the grave could offer. Death promised an infinity of peace, not the finite misery of an inactive life of confined torture, forever concealed from the life bearing shafts of the beloved rising sun. The orb that had been before taken for granted, yet now cherished above all else. To be forever refused further glimpses of the snow capped summits of the land of his birth, never again to witness the thrill of plundering unexplored lands beyond the crest of a bleeding horizon, and perhaps worst of all the denial to ever again encompass the lustful excitement of caressing the naked curves of the body of a trim yound wench.

This was indeed one of the buried chasms of Hell concealed within the inner depths of the palace's despised interior. A fearful ebony chamber devised to drive to the brinks of insanity the minds of the unfortunately condemned, through the inapt solitude of a limbo of listless dreary silence.

- 3½ -

A TIGHTLY RUNG ELLIPTICAL CIRCLE or torches cast their wavering shafts prancing morbidly over the smooth surface of a rectangular, ridged alter. Expertly chiseled the forms of grotesque gargoyles graced the oblique rim protruberating the length of the grim orifice of death, staring forever ahead into nothingness in complete ignorance of the bloody rites enacted in their prescence. Brown flaking stains decorated the golden surface of the ridge surrounding the alter, which banked to a small slit at the lower right hand corner of the altar. The slit stood above a crudely pounded pail which had several silver meshed chalices hanging at its sides. Dangling at the rimof golden mallet, the handle of which was engraved with images of twisted faces and groved at its far end with slots designed for a snug hand grip. The head of the mallet was slightly larger than a clenched fist and shaped into a smooth oval mass.

Encircling the marble altar was a congregation of leering shamen. Eerie chants of a bygone age, originating unknown eons before the memory of man, were being uttered from the buried recesses of the acolytes' deep lings. Orange paint was smeared in generous globules over the tops of thw Priests' wrinkled shaven scalps, while golden rings projected from the lobes of their pink ears. Ornate robes of lusciour purple satin enclosed their bulging torsos, attached around their waists with silvered silk lashes latched with ebony buckles in the shape of morose misshaped skulls. Dangling around their necks were oval fashoned medalions held by thin gold chains, featuring in their centers blood red rubys which resembled crimson fetish eyeballs. Cushoning their bare feet were plush red felt slippers with pointed golden spikes projecting from their tips.

Situated in front of the altar, and directly adjacent to the copper pail was a massive jade idol; a misshaped, hideous bust of the shamens' pagan diety. The shimmering green idol was placed in a sitting posture on an ornately carved golden throne raised upon a round, dvory plated dias; it bulging arms and webbed hands resting on the padded arms of the seat. Its head was entwined in golden snake -like coils hanging over its oblong ears, which tappered off to thin hollow points. Its nose was a bulging triangular mass, sunken in at its sides with tow gaping nostrils. Dramatic beneath the nostrils was a twisted, shaggy lipped mouth, giving the impression of a slovering sadistic grimace.

At the foot of the heathen diety a slender, pale faced female, naked but for a golden, jeweled harness enshrouding her huge outcropping breasts, supporting long silver laces which extended to her thigh, stood before the pearl white field with noticable shivers traveling up and down the length of her exquisitely molded body. Her delicate lips trembled beneath soft narrow hands as she attemped to conceal herself from the piercing stare of the ambivalent idol.

Glaring directly down towards her was the stoney, cycloptic face of the bloated diety. Gaping from its single obling socket was scintillating, many fauceted scarlet emerald, a brilliant gem seeming to possess a life all of its own. A priceless gleaming stone, capable of domineering the wealth of conquering empires...the eye of Argon.

- 4 -

ALL KNOWLEDGE OF MEASURING TIME had escaped Grignr. When a person is deprived of the sun, moon, and stars, he looses all conception of time as he had previously understood it. It seemed as if years had passed if time were being measured by terms of misery and mental anguish, yet he estimated that his stay had only been a few days in length. He has slept three times and had been fed five times since his awakening in the crypt. However, when the actions of the body are restricted its needs are also affected. The need for nourishmnet and slumber are directly proportional to the functions the body has performed, meaning that when free and active Grignr may become hungry every six hours and witness the desire for sleep every fifteen hours, whereas in his present condition he may encounter the need for food every ten hours , and the want for rest every twenty hours. All methods he had before depended upon were extinct in the dismal pit. Hence, he may have been imprisoned for ten minutes or ten years, he did not know, resulting in a disheartened emotion deep within his being.

The food, if you can honor the moldering lumps of fetid mush to that extent, was born to him by two guards who opened a portal at the top of his enclosure and shoved it to him in wooden bowls, retrieving the food and water bowels from his previous meal at the same time, after which they threw back the bolts on the iron latch and returned to their other duties. Since deprived of all other means of nourishment, Grignr was impelled to eat the tainted slop in order to ward off the paings of starvation, though as he stuffed it into his mouth with his filthy fingers and struggled to force it down his throat, he imagined it was that which had been spurned by the hounds stationed at various segments of the palace.

There was little in the baren vault that could occupy his body or mind. He had paced out the length and width of the enclosure time and time again and tested every granite slab which consisted the walls of the prison in hopes of finding a hidden passage to freedom, all of which was to no avail other than to keep him busy and distract his mind from wandering to thoughts of what he believed was his future. He had memorized the number of strides from one end to the other of the cell, and knew the exact number of slabs which made up the bleak dungeon. Numorous schemes were introduced and alternately discarded in turn as they succored to unravel to him no means of escape which stood the slightest chance of sucess.

Anguish continued to mount as his means of occupation were rapidly exhaus ted. Suddenly without no tive, he wasrouted from his contemplations as he detected a faint scratching sound at the end of the crypt opposite him. The sound seemed to be caused by something trying to scrape away at the grantite blocks the floor of the enclosure consisted of, the sandy scratching of something like an animal's claws.

Grignr gradually groped his way to the other end of the vault carefully feeling his way along with his hands ahead of him. When a few inches from the wall, a loud, penetrating squeal, and the scampering of small padded feet reverberated from the walls of the roughly hewn chamber.

Grignr threw his hands up to shield his face, and flung himself backwards upon his buttocks. A fuzzy form bounded to his hairy chest, burying its talons in his flesh while gnashing toward his throat with its grinding white teeth;its sour, fetid breath scortching the sqirming barbarians dilating nostrils. Grignr grappled with the lashing flexor muscles of the re-pugnant body of a garganuan brownhided rat, striv-ing to hold its razor teeth from his juicy jugular, as its beady grey organs of sight glazed into the flaring emeralds of its prey.

Taking hold of the rodent around its lean, growl-ing stomach with both hands Grignr pried it from his crimson rent breast, removing small patches of flayed flesh from his chest in the motion between the squalid black claws of the starving beast. Holding the rodent at arms length, he cupped his righthand over its frothing face, contrcting his fingers into a vice-like fist over the quivering head. Retaining his grips on the rat, grignr flexed his outstretched arms while slowly twisting his right hand clockwise and his left hand counter clockwise motion. The rodent let out a tortured squall, drawing scarlet as it violently dug its foam flecked fangs into the barbarians sweating palm, causing his face to contort to an ugly grimace as he cursed beneath his braeth.

With a loud crack the rodents head parted from its squirming torso, sending out a sprinking shower of crimson gore, and trailing a slimy string of dis-jointed vertebrae, snapped trachea, esophagus, and jugular, disjointed hyoid bone, morose purpled stretched hide, and blood seared muscles.

Flinging the broken body to the floor, Grignr shook his blood streaked hands and wiped them against his thigh until dry, then wiped the blood that had showered his face and from his eyes. Again sit-ting himself upon the jagged floor, he prepared to once more revamp his glum meditations. He told himself that as long as he still breathed the gust of life through his lungs, hope was not lost; he told himself this, but found it hard to comprehend in his gloomy surroundings. Yet he was still alive, his bulg-ing sinews at their peak of marvel, his struggling mind floating in a miral of impressed excellence of thought. Plot after plot sifted through his mind in energetic contemplations.

Then it hit him. Minutes may have passed in si-lent thought or days, he could not tell, but he stum-bled at last upon a plan that he considered as holding a slight margin of plausibility. He might die in the attempt, but he knew he would not submit without a final bloody struggle. It was not a foolproof plan, yet it built up a store of renewed vortexed energy in his overwroughtsoul, though he might perish in the exe-cution of the escape, he would still be escaping the life of infinite torture in store forhim. Either way he would still cheat the gloating prince of the succored revenge his sadistic mind craved so dearly.

The guards would soon come to bear him off to the prince's buried mines of dread, giving him the sought after opportunity to execute his newly formulated plan. Groping his way along the rough floor Grignr finally found his tool in a pool of congealed gore; the carcass of the decapitated rodent; the tool that the very filth he had been sentenced too, spawned. When the time came for action he would have to be prepared, so he set himself to rending the sticky hulk in grim silence, searching by the touch of his fingertips for the lever to freedom.

-5-

"UP TO THE ALTAR AND BE DONE WITH IT wench;" ordered a fidgeting shaman as he gave the female a grim stare accompanied by the wrinkling of his lips to a mirthful grin of delight.

The girl burst into a slow steady whimper, stooping shakily to her knees and cringing woefully from the priest with both arms wound snake-like around the bulging jade jade shin rising before her scantily attired figure. Her face was redly inflamed from the salty flow of tears spouting from her glassy dilated eyeballs.

With short, heavy footfals the priest approached the female, his piercing stare never wavering from her quivering young countenance. Halting before the terrified girl he projected his arm outward and motioned her to arise with an upward movement of his hand. the girl's whimpering increased slightly and she sunk closer to the floor rather than arising. The flickering torches outlined her trim build with a weird ornate glow as it cast a ghostly shadow dancing in horrid waves of splendor over smoothly worn whiteness of the marble hewn altar.

The shaman's lips curled back farther, exposing a set of blackened, decaying molars which transformed his slovenly grin into a wide greasy arc of sadistic mirth and alternately interposed into the female a strong sensation of stomach curdling nausea. "Have it as you will female;" gloated the enhanced priest as he bent over at the waist, projecting his ape-like arms forward, and clasped the female's slender arms with his hairy round fists. With an inward surge of of his biceps he harshly jerked the trembling girl to her feet and smothered her salty wet cheeks with the moldy touch of his decrepid, dull red lips.

The vile stench of the Shaman's hot fetid breath over came the nauseated female with a deep soul searing sickness, causing her to wrench her head backwards and regurgitate a slimy, orangewhite stream of swelling gore over the richly woven purple robe of the enthused acolyte.

The priest's lips trembled with a malicious rage as he removed his callous paws from the girl's arms and replaced them with tightly around her undulating neck, shaking her violently to and fro.

The girl gasped a tortured groan from her clamped lungs, her sea blue eyes bulging forth from damp sockets. Cocking her right foot backwards, she leashed it desperately outwards with the strength of a demon possessed, lodging her sandled foot squarely between the shaman's testicles.

The startled priest released his crushing grip, crimping his body over at the waist overlooking his recessed belly; wide open in a deep chasim. His face flushed to a rose red shade of crimson, eyelids fluttering wide with eyeballs protruding blindly outwards from their sockets to their outmost perimeters, while his lips quivered wildly about allowing an agonized wallow to gust forth as his breath billowed from burning lungs. His hands reached out clutching his urinary gland as his knees wobbled rapidly about for a few seconds then buckled, causing the ruptured shaman to collapse in an egg huddled mass to the granite pavement, rolling helplessly about in his agony.

The pathetic screeches of the shaman groveling in dejected misery upon the hand hewn granite laid pavement, worn smooth by countless hours of arduous sweat and toil, a welter of ichor oozing through his clenched hands, attracted the perturbed attention of his comrades from their foetid ulations. The actions of this this rebellious wench bespoke the creedence of an unheard of sacrilige. Never before in a lost maze of untold eons had a chosen one dared to demonstrate such blasphemy in the face of the cult's idolic diety.

The girl cowered in unreasoning terror, helpless in the face of the emblazoned acolytes' rage; her orchid tusseled face smothered betwixt her bulging bosom as she shut her curled lashed tightly hoping to open them and find herself awakening from a morbid nightmare. yet the hand of destiny decreed her no such mercy, the antagonized pack of leering shaman converging tensely upon her prostrate form were entangled all too lividly in the grim web of reality.

Shuddering from the clamy touch of the shaman as they grappled with her supple form,hands wrenching at her slender arms and legs in all directions, her bare body being molested in the midst of a labyrnth of orange smudges, purpled satin, and mangled skulls, shadowed in an eerie crimson glow; her confused head reeled then clouded in a mist of enshrouding ebony as she lapsed beneath the protective sheet of unconsiousness to a land peach and resign.

-6-

"TAKE HOLD OF THIS ROPE," said the first soldier, "and climb out from your pit, slut. Your presence is requested in another far deeper hell hole."

Grignr slipped his right hand to his thigh, concealing a small opaque object beneath the folds of the g-string wrapped about his waist. Brine wells swelled in Grignr's cold , jade squinting eyes, which grown accustomed to the gloom of the stygian pools of ebony engulfing him, were bedazzled and blinded by flickerer -ing radiance cast forth by the second soldiers's resin torch.

Tightly gripped in the second soldier's right hand, opposite the intermittent torch, was a large double edged axe, a long leather wound oaken handled transfixing the center of the weapon's iron head. Adorning the torso's of both of the sentries were thin yet sturdy hauberks, the breatplates of which were woven of tightly hemmed twines of reinforced silver braiding. Cupping the soldiers' feet were thick leather sandals, wound about their shins to two inches below their knees.

Wrapped about their waists were wide satin girdles, with slender bladed poniards dangling loosely from them, the hilts of which featured scarlet encrusted gems. Resting upon the manes of their heads, and reaching midway to their brows were smooth copper morions. Spiraling the lower portion of the helmet were short, upcurved silver spikes, while a golden hump spired from the top of each basinet. Beneath their chins, wound around their necks, and draping their clad shoulders dangled regal purple satin cloaks, which flowed midway to the soldiers feet.

hand over hand, feet braced against the dank walls of the enclosure, huge Grignr ascended from the moldering dephs of the forlorn abyss. His swelled limbs, stiff due to the boredom of a timeless inactivity, compounded by the musty atmosture and jagged granite protuberan against his body, craved for action. The opportunity now presenting itself served the purpose of oiling his rusty joints, and honing his dulled senses.

He braced himself, facing the second soldier. The sentry's stature was was wildly exaggerated in the glare of the flickering cresset cuppex in his right fist. His eyes were wide open in a slightly slanted owlish glaze, enhanced in their sinister intensity by the hawk-bill curve of his nose andpale yellow pique of his cheeks.

"Place your hands behind your back," said the second soldier as he raised his ax over his right shoulder blade and cast it a wavering glance. "We must bind your wrists to parry any attempts at escape. Be sure to make the knot a stout one, Broig, we wouldn't want our guest to take leave of our guidance."

Broig grasped Grignr's left wrist and reached for the barbarians's right wrist. Grignr wrenched his right arm free and swilveledswilveled to face Broig, reachbeneath his loin cloth with his right hand. The sentry grappled at his girdle for the sheathed dagger, but recoiled short of his intentions as Grignr's right arm swept swept to his gorge. The soldier went limp, his bobbing eyes rolling beneath fluttering eyelids, a deep welt across his spouting gullet. Without lingering to observe the result of his efforts, Grignr dropped to his knees. The second soldier's axe cleft over Grignr's head in a blze of silvered ferocity, severing several scarlet locks from his scalp. Coming to rest in his fellow's stomach, the iron head crashed through mail and flesh with splintering force, spilling a pool of crimsoned entrails over the granite paving.

Before the sentry could wrench his axe free from his comrade's carcass, he found Grignr's massive hands clasped about his throat, choking the life from his clamped lungs. With a zealous grunt, the Ecordian flexed his tightly corded biceps, forcing the grim faced soldier to one knee. The sentry plunged his right fist into Grignr's face, digging his grimy nails into the barbarians flesh. Ejaculating a curse through rasping teeth, grignr surged the bulk of his weight foreard,bowling the beseiged soldier over upon his back. The sentry's arms collapsed to his thigh, shuddering convulsively; his bulging eyes staring blindly from a bloated ,cherry red face.

Rising to his feet, Grignr shook the bllod from his eyes, ruffling his surly red mane as a brush fire swaying to the nightime breeze. Stooping over the spr sprawled corpse of the first soldier, Grignr retrieved a small white object from a pool of congealing gore. Snorting a gusty billow of mirth, he once more concealed th e tiny object beneath his loin cloth; the tediously honed pelvis bone of the broken rodent. Returning his attention toward the second soldier, Grignr turned to the task of attiring his limbs. To move about freely through the dim recesses of the castle would require the grotesque garb of its soldiery.

Utilizing the silence and stealth aquired in the untamed climbs of his childhood, Grignr slink through twisting corridors, and winding stairways, lighting his way with the confisticated torch of his dispatched guardian. Knowing where his steps were leading to, Grignr meandered aimlessly in search of an exit from the chateau's dim confines. The wild blood coarsing through his veins yearned for the undefiled freedom of the livid wilderness lands.

Coming upon a fork in the passage he treaked, voices accompanied by clinking footfalls discerned to his sensitive ears from the left corridor. Wishing to avoid contact, Grignr veered to the right passageway. If aquested as to the purpose of his presence, his barbarous accent would reveal his identity, being that his attire was not that of the castle's mercenary troops.

In grim silence Grignr treaded down the dingily lit corridor; a stalking panther creeping warily along on padded feet. After an interminable period of wandering through the dull corridors; no gaps to break the monotony of the cold gray walls, Grignr espied a small winding stairway. Descending the flight of arced granite slabs to their posterior, Grignr was confronted by a short haalway leading to a tall arched wooden doorway.

Halting before the teeming portal portal, Grignr restes his shaggy head sideways against the barrier. Detecting no sounds from within, he grasped the looped metel handle of the door; his arms surging with a tremendous effort of bulging muscles, yet the door would not budge. Retrieving his ax from where he had sheathed it beneath his girdle, he hefted it in his mighty hands with an apiesed grunt, and wedging one of its blackened edges into the crack between the portal and its iron rimed sill. Bracing his sandaled right foot against the rougjly hewn wall, teeth tightly clenched, Grignr appilevered the oaken haft, employing it as a lever whereby to pry open the barrier. The leather wound hilt bending to its utmost limits of endurance, the massive portal swung open with a grating of snapped latch and rusty iron hinges.

Glancing about the dust swirled room in the gloomily dancing glare of his flickering cresset, Grignr eyed evidences of the enclosure being nothing more than a forgotten storeroom. Miscellaneous articles required for the maintainance of a castle were piled in disorganized heaps at infrequent intervals toward the wall opposite the barbarian's piercing stare. Utilizing long, bounding strides, Grignr paced his way over to the mounds of supplies to discover if any articles of value were contained within their midst.

Detecting a faint clinking sound, Grignr sprawled to his left side with the speed of a striking cobra, landing harshly upon his back; torch and axe loudly clattering to the floor in a morass of sparks and flame. A elmwoven board leaped from collapsed flooring, clashing against the jagged flooring and spewing a shower x of orange and yellow sparks over Grignr's startled face. Rising uneasily to his feet, the half stunned Ecordian glared down at the grusome arm of death he had unwittingly sprung. "Mrifk!"

If not for his keen auditory organs and lighting steeled reflexes, Grignr would have been groping through the shadowed hell-pits of the Grim Reaper. He had unknowingly stumbled upon an ancient, long forgotton booby trap; a mistake which would have stunted the perusal of longevity of one less agile. A mechanism, similar in type to that of a minature catapult was concealed beneath two collapsable sections of granite flooring. The arm of the device was four feet long, boasting razor like cleats at regular intervals along its face with which it was to skewer the luckless body of its would be victim. Grignr had stepped upon a concealed catch which relaesed a small metal latch beneath the two granite sections, causing them to fall inward, and thereby loose the spiked arm of death they precariously held in .

Partially out of curiosity and partially out of an inordinate fear of becoming a pincushion for a possible second trap, Grignr plunged his torch into the exposed gap in the floor. The floor of a second chamber stood out seven feet below the glare. Tossing his torch through the aperature, Grignr grasped the side of an adjoining tile, dropping down.

Glancing about the room, Grignr discovered that he had decended into the palace's mausoleum. Rectangular stone crypts cluttered the floor at evenly placed intervals. The tops of the enclosures were plated with thick layers of virgin gold, while the sides were plated with white ivory; at one time sparkling, but now grown dingy through the passage of the rays of allencompassing mother time. Featured at the head of each sarcophagus in tarnished silver was an expugnisively carved likeness of its rotting inhabitant.

A dingy atmosphere pervaded the air of the chamber; which sealed in the enclosure for an unknown period had grown thick and stale. Intermingling with the curdled currents was the repugnant stench of slowly moldering flesh, creeping ever slowly but surely through minute cracks in the numerous vaults. Due to the embalming of the bodies, their flesh decayed at a much slower rate than is normal, yet the nauseous oder was none the less repellant.

Towering over Grignr's head was the trap he released. The mechanism of the miniaturized catapolt was cluttered with mildew and cobwebs. Notwithstanding these relics of antiquity, its efficiency remained unimpinged. To the right of the trap wound a short stairway through a recession in the ceiling; a concealed entrance leading to the mausoleum for which the catapult had obviously been erected as a silent, relentless guardian.

Climbing up the side of the device, Grignr set to the task of resetting its mechanism. In the e event that a search was organized, it would prove well to leave no evidence of his presence open to wandering eyes. Besides , it might even serve to dwindle the size of an opposing force.

Descending from his perch, Grignr was startled by a faintly muffled scream of horrified desperation. His hair prickled yawkishly in disorganized clumps along his scalp. As a cold danced along the length of his spinal cord. No moral/mortal barrier, human or otherwise, was capable of arousing the numbing sensation of fear inside of Grignr's smoldering soul. However, he was overwrought by the forces of the barbarians' instinctive fear of the supernatural. His mighty thews had always served to adequately conquer any tangible foe., but the intangible was something distant and terrible. Dim horrifying tales passed by word of mouth over glimmering camp fires and skins of wine had more than once served the purpose of chilling the marrowed core of his sturdy limbed bones.

Yet, the scream contained a strangely human quality, unlike that which Grignr imagined would come from the lungs of a demon or spirit, making Grignr take short nervous strides advancing to the sarcophagus from which the sound was issuing. Clenching his teeth in an attempt to steel his jangled nerves, Grignr slid the engraved slab from the vault with a sharp rasp of grinding stone. Another long drawn cry of terror infested anguish met the barbarian, scoring like the shrill piping of a demented banshee; piercing the inner fibres of his superstitious brain with primitive dread dread and awe.

Stooping over to espy the tomb's contents, the glittering Ecordians nostrills were singed by the scorching aroma of a moldering corpse, long shut up and fermenting; the same putrid scent which permeated the entire chamber, though multiplied to a much more concentrated dosage. The shriveled, leathery packet of crumbling bones and dried flacking flesh offered no resistance, but remained in a fixed position of perpetual vigilance, watching over its dim abode from hollow gaping sockets.

The tortured crys were not coming from the tomb but from some hidden depth below ! Pulling the reaking corpse from its resting place, Grignr tossed it to the floor in a broken, mangled heap. Upon one side of the crypt's bottom was attach -ed a series of tiny hinges while running parallel along the opposite side of a convex railing like protruberance; laid so as to appear as a part of the interior surface of the sarcophagus.

Raising the slab upon its bronze hinges, long removed from the gaze of human eyes, Grignr percieved a scene which caused his blood to smolder not unlike bubbling, molten lava. Directly below him a whimpering female lay stretched upon a smooth surfaced marble altar. A pack of grasy faced shamen clustered around her in a tight circular formation. Crouched over the girl was a tall, potbellied priest; his face dominated by a disgusting, open mouthed grimace of sadistic glee. Suspended from the acolyte's clenched right hand was a carven oval faced mallet, which he waved menacingly over the girl's shadowed face; an incoherent gibberish flowing from his grinning, thick lipped mouth.

In the face of the amorphos, broad breated female, stretched out aluringly before his gaping eyes; the universal whim of nature filing a plea of despair inside of his white hot soul; Grignr acted in the only manner he could perceive. Giving vent to a hoarse, throat rending battle cry, Grignr plunged into the midst of the startled shamen; torch simmering in his left hand andax twirling in his right hand.

A gaunt skull faced priest standing at the far side of the altar clutched desperately at his throat, coughing furiously in an attempt to catch his breath. Lurching helplessly to and fro, the acolyte pitched headlong against the gleaming base of a massive jade idol. Writhing agonizedly against the hideous image, foam flecking his chalk white lips, the priest struggled helplessly - - -the victim of an epileptic siezure.

Startled by the barbarians stunning appearance, the chronic fit of their fellow, and the fear that Grignr might be the avantgarde of a conquering force dedicated to the cause of destroying their degenerated cult, the saman momentarily lost their composure. Giving vent to heedless pandemonium, the priests fell easy prey to Grignr's sweeping arc of crimsoned death and maiming distruction.

The acolyte performing the sacrifice took a vicious blow to the stomach; hands clutching vitals and severed spinal cord as he sprawled over the altar. The disor anized priests lurched and staggered with split skulls, dismembered limbs, and spewing entrails before the enraged Ecordian's relentless onslaught. The howles of the maimed and dying reverberated against the walls of the tiny chamber; a chorus of hell frought despair; as the granite floor ran red with blood. The entire chamber was encompassed in the heat of raw savage butchery as Grignr luxuriated in the grips of a primitive, beastly blood lust.

Presently all went silenet save for the ebbing groans of the sinking shaman and Grignr's heaving breath accompanied by several gusty curses. The well had run dry. No more lambs remained for the slaughter.

The rampaging stead of death having taken of Grignr for the moment, left the barbarian free to the exploitation of his other perusials. Towering over his head was the misshaped image of the cult's hideous diety - - - Argon. The fantastic size of the idol in consideration of its being of pure jade was enough to cause the senses of any man to stagger and reel, yet thus was not the case for the behemoth. he had paid only casual notice to this incredible fact, while riviting the whole of his attention upon the jewel protruding from the idol's sole socket; its masterfully cut faucets emitting blinding rays of hypnotising beauty. After all, a man cannot slink from a heavily guarded palace while burdened down by the intense bulk of a squatting statue, providing of course that the idol can even be hefted, which in fact was beyond the reaches of Grignr's coarsing stamina. On the other hand, the jewel, gigantic as it was, would not present a hinderence of any mean concern.

"Help me ... please ... I can make it well worth your while," pleaded a soft, anguish strewn voice wafting over Grignr's shoulders as he plucked the dull red emerald from its roots. Turning, Grignr faced the female that had lured him into this blood bath, but whom had become all but forgotten in the heat of the battle.

"You"; ejaculated the Ecordian in a pleased tone. "I though that I had seen the last of you at the tavern, but verilly I was mistaken." Grignr advanced into the grips of the female's entrancing stare, severing the golden chains that held her captive upon the altars highly polished face of ornamental limestone.

As Grignr lifted the girl from the altar, her arms wound dexterously about his neck; soft and smooth against his harsh exterior. "Art thou pleased that we have chanced to meet once again?" Grignr merely voiced an sighed grunt, returning the damsels embrace while he smothered her trim, delicate lips between the coursing protrusions of his reeking maw.

"Let us take leave of this retched chamber." Stated Grignr as he placed the female upon her feet. She swooned a moment, causing Grignr to giver her support then regained her stance. "Art thou able to find your way through the accursed passages of this castle? Mrifk! Every one of the corridors of this damned place are identical."

"Aye; I was at one time a slave of prince Agaphim. His clammy touch sent a sour swill through my belly, but my efforts reaped a harvest. I gained the pig's liking whereby he allowed me the freedom of the palace. It was through this means that I eventually managed escape of the palace . . . . it was a simple matter to seduce the sentry at the western gate. His trust found him with a dagger thrust his ribs," the wench stated whimsicoracally.

"What were you doing at the tavern whence I discovered you?" asked Grignr as he lifted the female through the opening into the mausoleum. "I had sought to lay low from the palace's guards as they conducted their search for me. The tavern was seldom frequented by the palace guards and my identity was unknown to the common soldiers. It was through the disturbance that you caused that the palace guards were attracted to the tavern. I was dragged away shortly after you were escorted to the palace."

"What are you called by female?"

"Carthena, daughter of Minkardos, Duke of Barwego, whose lands border along the northwestern fringes of Gorzom. I was paid as homage to Agaphim upon his thirty-eighth year,"husked the femme !

"And I am called a barbarian!" Grunted Grignr in a disgusted tone !

"Aye! The ways of our civilization are in many ways warped and distorted, but what is your calling," she queried , bustily?

"Grignr of Ecordia."

"Ah, I have heard vaguely of Ecordia. It is the hill country to the far east of the Noregolean Empire. I have also heard Agaphim curse your land more than once when his troops were routed in the unaccustomed mountains and gorges."Sayeth she.

"Aye. My people are not tarnished by petty luxuries and baubles. They remain fierce and unconquerable in their native climes." After reaching the hidden panel at the head of the stairway, Grignr was at a loss in regard to its operation. His fiercest heaves were as pebbles against burnished armour! Carthena depressed a small symbol included within the elaborate design upon the panel whereopen it slowly slid into a cleft in the wall. "How did you come to be the victim of those crazed shamen?" Quested Grignr as he escorted Carthena through the piles of rummage on the left side of the trap.

"By A aphim's orders I was thrust into a secluded cell to await his passing of sentence. By some means, the Priests of Argon acquired a set of keys to the cell. They slew the guard placed over me and abducted me to the chamber in which you chanced to come upon the scozsctic sacrifice. Their hell-spawned cult demands a sacrifice once every three moons upon its full journey through the heavens. They were startled by your unannounced appearance through the fear that you had been sent by Agaphim. The prince would surely have submitted them to the most ghastly of tortures if he had ever discovered their unfaithfulness to Sargon, his bastard diety. Many of the partakers of the ritual were high nobles and high trustees of the inner palace; Agaphim's pittiless wrath would have been unparalled."

"They have no more to fear of Agaphim now!" Bellowed Grignr in a deep mirthful tome; a gleeful smirk upon his face. "I have seen that they were delivered from his vengence."

Engrossed by Carthena's graceful stride and conversation Grignr failed to take note of the footfalls rapidly approaching behind him. As he swung aside the arched portal linking the chamber with the corridors beyond, a maddened, blood lusting screech reverberated from his ear drums. Seemingly utilizing the speed of thought, Grignr swiveled to face his unknown foe. With gaping eyes and widened jaws, Grignr raised his axe above his surly mein; but he was too late.

-7-

WITH WOBBLING KNEES and swimming head, the priest that had lapsed into an epileptic siezure rose unsteadily to his feet. While enacting his choking fit in writhing agony, the shaman was overlooked by Grignr. The barbarian had mistaken the siezure for the death throes of the acolyte, allowing the priest to avoid his stinging blade. The sight that met the priests inflamed eyes nearly served to sprawl him upon the floor once more. The sacrificial sat it grim, blood splattered silence all around him, broken only by the occasional yelps and howles of his maimed and butchered fellows. Above his head rose the hideous idol, its empty socket holding the shaman's ifurbished infuriated gaze. His eyes turned to a stoney glaze with the realization of the pillage and blasphemy. Due to his high succeptibility following the siezure, the priest was transformed into a raving maniac bent soley upon reaking vengeance. With lips curled and quivering, a crust of foam dripping from them, the acolyte drew a long, wicked looking jewel hilted scimitar from his silver girdle and fled through the aperature in the ceiling uttering a faintly perceptible ceremonial jibberish.

-7½-

A SWEEPING SCIMITAR swung towards Grignr's head in a shadowed blur of motion. With Axe raised over his head, Grignr prepared to parry the blow, while gaping wideeyed in open mouthed perplexity. Suddenly a sharp snap resounded behind the frothing shaman. The scimitar, halfway through its fatal sweep, dropped from a quivering nerveless hand, clattering harmlessly to the stoneage. Cutting his screech short with a bubbling, red mouthed gurgle, the lacerated acolyte staggered under the pressure of the released spring-board. After a moment of hopeless struggling, the shaman buckled, sprawling face down in a widening pool of bllod and entrails, his regal purple robe blending enhancingly with the swirling streams of crimson.

"Mrifk! I thought I had killed the last of those dogs;" muttered Grignr in a half apathetic state.

"Nay Grignr. You doubtless grew careless while giving vent to your lusts. But let us not tarry any long lest we over tax the fates.The paths leading to freedom will soon be barred. The wretch's crys must certainly have attracted unwanted attention," the wench mused.

"By what direction shall we pursue our flight? ,"

"Up that stair and down the corridor a short distance is the concealed enterance to a tunnel seldom used by others than the prince, and known to few others save the palace's royalty. It is used mainly by the prince when he wishes to take leave of the palace in secret. It is not always in the Prince's best interests to leave his chateau in public view. Even while under heavy guard he is often assaulted by hurtling stones and rotting fruits. The commoners have little love for him." lectured the nerelady!

"It is amazing that they would ever have left a pig like him become their ruler. I should imagine that his people would rise up and crucify him like the dog he is."

"Alas, Grignr, it is not as simple as all that. His soldiers are well paid by him. So long as he keeps their wages up they will carry out his damned wishes. The crude impliments of the commonfolk would never stand up under an onslaught of forged blades and protective armor; they would be going to their own slaughter," stated Carthena to a confused, but angered Grignr as they topped the stairway.

"Yet how can they bear to live under such oppression? I would sooner die beneath the sword than live under such a dog's command." added Grignr as the pair stalked down the hall in the direction opposite that in which Grignr had come.

"But all men are not of the same mold that you are born of, they choose to live as they are so as to save their filthy necks from the chopping block." Returned Carthena in a disgusted tone as she cast an appiesed glance towards the stalwart figure at her side whose left arm was wound dextrously about her slim waist; his slowly waning torch casting their images in intermingling wisps as it dangled from his left hand.

Presently Carthena came upon the panel, concealed amongst the other granite slabs and discernable only by the burned out cresset above it. "As I push the cresset aside push the panel inwards." Catrhena motioned to the panel she was refering to and twisted the cresset in a counterclockwise motion. Grignr braced his right shoulder against the walling, concentrating the force of his bulk against it. The slab gradually swung inward with a slight grating sound. Carthena stooped beneath Grignr's corded arms and crawled upon all fours into the passage beyond. Grignr followed after easing the slab back into place.

Winding before the pair was a dark musty tunnel, exhibiting tangled spider webs from it ceiling to wall and an oozing, sickly slime running lazily upon its floor. Hanging from the chipped wall upon GrignR's right side was a half mouldered corpse, its grey flacking arms held in place by rusted iron manacles. Carthena flinched back into Grignr's arms at sight of the leering set in an ugly distorted grimmace; staring horribly at her from hollow gaping sockets.

"This alcove must also be used by Agaphim as a torture chamber. I wonder how many of his enemies have disappeared into these haunts never to be heard from again," pondered the hulking brute.

"Let us flee before we are also caught within Agaphim's ghastly clutches. The exit from this tunnel cannot be very far from here!" Said Carthena with a slight sob to her voice, as she sagged in Grignr's encompasing embrace.

"Aye; It will be best to be finished with this corridor as soon as it is possible. But why do you flinch from the sight of death so? Mrift! You have seen much death this day without exhibiting such emotions." Exclaimed Grignr as he led her trembling form along the dingy confines.

"---The man hanging from the wall was Doyanta. He had committed the folly of showing affections for me in front of Agaphim --- he never meant any harm by his actions!" At this Carthena broke into a slow steady whimpering, chokking her voice with gasping sobs. "There was never anything between us yet Agaphim did this to him! The beast! May the demons of Hell's deepest haunts claw away at his wretched flesh for this merciless act!" she prayed.

"I detect that you felt more for this fellow than you wish to let on ... but enough of this, We can talk of such matters after we are once more free to do so." With this Grignr lifted the grieved female to her feet and strode onward down the corridor, supporting the bulk of her weight with his surging left arm.

Presently a dim light was perceptibly filtering into the tunnel, casting a dim reddish hue upon the moldy wall of the passage's grim confines. Carthena had ceased her whimpering and partially regained her composure. "The tunnel's end must be nearing. Rays of sunlight are beginning to seep into ..."

Grignr clameed his right hand over Carthena's mouth and with a slight struggle pulled her over to the shadows at the right hand wall of the path, while at the same time thrusting this torch beneath an overhanging stone to smother its flickering rays. "Be silent; I can hear footfalls approaching through the tunnel;" growled Grignr in a hushed tone.

"All that you hear are the horses corraled at the far end of the tunnel. That is a further sign that we are nearing our goal." She stated!

"All that you hear is less than I hear! I heard footsteps coming towards us. Silence yourself that we may find out whom we are being brought into contact with. I doubt that any would have thought as yet of searching this passage for us. The advantage of surprize will be upon our side." Grignr warned.

Carthena cast her eyes downward and ceased any further pursuit towards conversation, an irritating habit in which she had gained an amazing proficiency. Two figures came into the pairs view, from around a turn in the tunnel. They were clothed in rich luxuriant silks and rambling o on in conversation while ignorant of their crouching foes waiting in an ambush ahead.

"...That barbarian dog is cringing beneath the weight of the lash at this very moment sire. He shall cause no more disturbance."

"Aye, and so it is with any who dare to cross the path of Sargon's chosen one." said the 2nd man.

"But the peasants are showing signs of growing unrest. They complain that they cannot feet their families while burdened with your taxes."

"I shall teach those sluts the meaning of humility! Order an immediate increase upon their taxes. They dare to question my sovereign authority, Ha-a, they shall soon learn what true oppression can be . I will ... "

A shodowed bulk leapt from behind a jutting promontory as it brought down a double edged axe with the spped of a striking thought. One of the nobles sagged lifeless to the ground, skull split to the teeth.

Grignr gasped as he observed the bisected face set in its leering death agonies. It was Agafnd! The dead mans comrade having recovered from his shock drew a jewel encrusted dagger from beneath the folds of his robe and lunged toward the barbarians back. Grignr spun at the sound from behind and smashed down his crimsoned axe once more. His antagonist lunged howling to a stream of stagnent green water, grasping a spouting stump that had once been a wrist. Grignr raised his axe over his head and prepaired to finish the incomplete job, but was detered half way through his lunge by a frenzied screech from behind.

Carthena leapt to the head of the writhing figure, plunging a smoldering torch into the agonized face. The howls increased in their horrid intensity, stifled by the sizzling of roasting flesh, then died down until the man was reduced to a blubbering mass of squirming, insensate flesh.

Grignr advance to Carthena's side wincing slightly from the putrid aroma of charred flesh that rose in a puff of thick white smog throughout the chamber. Carthena reeled slightly, staring dasedly downward at her gruesome handywork. "I had to do it ... it was Agaphim ... I had to, " she exclaimed!

"Sargon should be more carful of his right hand men." Added Grignr, a smug grin upon his lips. "But to hell with Sargon for now, the stench is becoming bother-some to me." With that Grignr grasped Carthena around the waist leading her around the bend in the cave and into the open.

A ball of feral red was rising through the mists of the eastern horizon, dissipating the slinking shadows of the night. A coral stood before the pair, enclosing two grazing mares. Grignr reached into a weighted down leather pouch dangling at his side and drew forth the scintillant red emerald he had obtained from the bloated idol. Raising it toward the sun he said, "We shall do well with bauble,eh!"

Carthena gaped at the gem gasping in a terrified manner "The eye of Argon, Oh! Kalla!" At this the gem gave off a blinding glow, then dribbled through Grignr's fingers in a slimy red ooze. Grignr stepped back, pushing Carthena behind him. The droplets of slime slowly converged into a pulsating jelly-like mass. A single opening transfixed the blob, forminf into a leechlike maw.

Then the hideous transgressor of nature flowed towards Grignr, a trail of greenish slime lingering behind it. The single gap puckered repeatedly emitting a ghastly sucking sound.

Grignr spread his legs into a battle stance, steeling his quivering thews for a battle royal with a thing he knew not how to fight. Carthena wound her arms about her protectors neck, mumbling, "Kill it! Kill!"While her entire body trembled.

The thing was almost upon Grignr when he buried his axe into the gristly maw. It passed through the blob and clanged upon the ground. Grignr drew his axe back with a film of yellow-green slime clinging to the blade. The thing was seemingly unaffected. Then it started to slooze up his leg. The hairs upon his nape stoode on end from the slimey feel of the things buly, bulk. The Nautous sucking sound became louder, and Grignr felt the blood being drawn from his body. With each hiss of hideous pucker the thing increased in size.

Grignr shook his foot about madly in an attempt to dislodge the blob, but it clung like a leech, still feeding upon his rapidly draining life fluid. He grasped with his hands trying to rip it off, but only found his hands entangled in a sickly gluelike substance. The slimey thing continued its puckering ; now having grown the size of Grignr's leg from its vampiric feast.

Grignr began to reel and stagger under the blob, his chalk white face and faltering muscles attesting to the gigantic loss of blood. Carthena slipped from Grignr in a death-like faint, a morrow chilling scream upon her red rubish lips. In final desperation Grignr grasped the smoldering torch upon the ground and plunged it into the reeking maw of the travesty. A shudder passed through the thing. Grignr felt the blackness closing upon his eyes, but held on with the last ebb of his rapidly waning vitality. He could feel its grip lessoning as a hideous gurgling sound erupted from the writhing maw. The jelly like mass began to bubble like a vat of boiling tar as quavers passed up and down its entire form.

With a sloshing plop the thing fell to the ground, evaporating in a thick scarlet cloud until it reatained its original size. It remained thus for a moment as the puckered maw took the shape of a protruding red eyeball, the pupil of which seemed to unravel before it the tale of creation. How a shapeless mass slithered from the quagmires of the stygmatic pool of time, only to degenerate into a leprosy of avaricious lust. In that fleeting moment the grim mystery of life was revealed before Grignr's ensnared gaze.

The eyeballs glare turned to a sudden plea of mercy, a plea for the whole of humanity. Then the blob began to quiver with violent convulsions; the eyeball shattered into a thousand tiny fragments and evaporated in a curling wisp of scarlet mist. The very ground below the thing began to vibrate and swallow it up with a belch.

The thing was gone forever. All that remained was a dark red blotch upon the face of the earth, blotching things up. Shaking his head, his shaggy mane to clear the jumbled fragments of his mind, Grignr tossed the limp female over his shoulder. Mounting one of the disgruntled mares, and leading the other; the weary, scarred barbarian trooted slowly off into the horizon to become a tiny pinpoint in a filtered filed of swirling blue mists, leaving the Nobles, soldiers and peasants to replace the missing monarch. Long leave the king ! ! ! !

by Jim Theis
winner of the Jay T. Rikosh award for excellence!

52747148R00098

Made in the USA
Columbia, SC
06 March 2019